SIGHT UNSEEN

The Haunting Of Blackstone Manor

James M. Matheson

Aberdeenshire Publishing

Phoenix, Arizona

Aberdeenshire Publishing
Box 1306
Litchfield Park, Arizona 85340
www.jamesmmatheson.com

Publisher's Note: This is a work of fiction. Names, characters, places, and incidents are a product of the author's imagination. Locales and public names are sometimes used for atmospheric purposes. Any resemblance to actual people, living or dead, or to businesses, companies, events, institutions, or locales is completely coincidental.

Sight Unseen. James M. Matheson. -- 1st ed.

Gratitude and thanks to

Allen and Ellie DeEver

CONTENTS

CHAPTER ONE

Scratch scratch scratch. Scratch scratch. Silence. Scratch scratch scratch.

Katie flung off her sheets and jumped to her feet by the side of the bed. At 4:44 AM, she'd had enough.

"I'm gonna get you little buggers and send you back to your maker!"

She stormed out the bedroom door into the dimly lit hallway, grabbed a 6-foot 2×4 that was lying in the hallway and rammed it hard into the ceiling. The little noisemakers scrambled in every direction back to their hiding spots.

Unfortunately, Katie was now covered in ceiling dust.

"Fabulous," she said sarcastically. "Not like I damaged anything."

Katie suddenly broke out in laughter. It was an old home, and the ceiling in the hallway had all but fallen in. The mice had probably saved her money because the contractors would have less of it to pull down.

The old floors creaked as she headed back to her bedside table. She picked up her phone and dictated a message to herself: "Reminder: Pick up mouse... and rattraps."

***

Sunlight flooded the huge old-fashioned kitchen. It was easily one of the two best-looking rooms in the old house. Sure, it needed restoration work and a considerable amount of paint, but it remained glorious.

Katie enjoyed a bowl of porridge and a pot of tea. It took no time at all for her to put the dishes in the sink and head to the family room to see what was behind the wallpaper.

Everything in this house was big and bright. The family room was no exception. Except for the horrible wallpaper.

Katie approached the job with a bit of dread, but she was surprised at how easily the wallpaper came off. It was almost like a snake shedding its skin. *Probably due to the house having been vandalized*, she thought to herself.

Many years ago vandals had broken into the shuttered home, smashing out all the windows, spray-painting vulgar comments on the walls and destroying several old paintings. Rain and snow had then damaged the room and the floor.

"Mold. Great. Hopefully manageable," she said to herself. She had a lifelong habit of talking to herself. Narrating, as she called it. Drove her friends and family nuts. "I better make a note of—"

A show tune started playing loudly from the kitchen. It was her cell phone. She dropped her tools and rushed to the kitchen trying to get it before it went to voicemail.

The phone display said 'MEL.' Her best friend.

"Hey, chickie! How are you?" said Katie.

"Fabulous. Did you get a good night's rest last night?"

"God, no. My friends kept me up again. I'd just get to sleep and then just as I start to doze off they get to their scratching."

"Maybe it's a ghost..."

"Yeah, well, if it is a ghost he poops tiny pellets all around the attic!"

They both broke out in laughter.

"So, any regrets about moving down from Seattle to Colorado?" Mel asked.

"Not at all. This will be, hands down, my most profitable flip thanks to you finding it for me. The bones of this house are incredible, it just needs a massive cosmetic update. If I could—"

Mel interrupted, as she was prone to do. "Has the creepy owner been by at all?"

"Yes. Mr. Watkin was by yesterday. He's a pretty nice guy actually, once you get to know him. He just seems to be devoid of emotion—"

"Devoid? You been reading the dictionary again?"

Katie ignored the jab. "He seems so relieved to have gotten rid of the place. I'm happy for him, but happier for me! I gotta say, though, he seems to have money. I still can't figure out why he sold it so cheap."

"Well, rumors have it that he was—or is—ill and just couldn't keep it up. Other rumors said he lost his job and couldn't afford the upkeep. Who knows... and who cares? Finders keepers."

"Well, I like to think of it as win-win, but yeah, I'm going to do great with this. Hey, when are you coming to help?"

"I'll be there tonight as promised. Just have to finish up another real estate deal. Five-ish?"

"Thank goodness. It will be great having some company. New contractor coming this afternoon. Too bad the other guy flaked on me, he was hot!"

"Single? Nice buns?"

"Who cares. Couldn't commit to a job, so what good would he be in a relationship?"

"I'm just looking for some tail—"

"Bye, Mel! Take a cold shower and I'll see you tonight."

As Katie was hanging up, she heard a vehicle pull up out front. Walking to the library she saw a huge black pickup with ridiculously oversized wheels come to a stop. An equally large man stepped down, first to a silver side rail and then to the ground. The new contractor had arrived: "Big" John Magnuson. Right on time. Refreshing, as the other contractor was useless.

Katie scrambled back to the kitchen to grab her sweater. It was warm in the house, but wearing a white t-shirt and no bra, she wanted to cover up her 'damned headlights.' Her boobs were both a blessing and a curse.

Swinging open the front door she caught Big John with his large hand in a fist, just about to knock. They both chuckled as he stood frozen in the pose in the doorway.

"Ms. Pearson?"

"Katie. You must be Big John?"

"Yes, Ma'am," he said. An imposing figure, he stood 6'6" and his face looked weathered.

"Come on in, John, would you like a coffee?"

"That'd be great, Ma'am."

"The kitchen is probably best. Let's go grab a seat in there and figure stuff out."

The kitchen had original alternating black and white tiles, white cupboards and a multitude of windows making it bright and airy. An antique table sat in the center with mismatched painted white chairs. John sat in one while Katie got the coffee maker going.

"When I was a kid we thought this place was haunted. Too bright and warm for spooky ghosts to haunt," John said. He laughed.

"Did you have friends here, John? Have you been in the house before?"

"Uh... no, no friends. House belonged to the Blackstone family, but nobody has ever really lived here in years. I think people come and maybe house-sit, or maybe use it like a cottage to stay short term, but that'd be about it..."

Katie sensed he was reflecting on something and gently pressed again. "Have you been in here before?"

"Well. I'd be lyin' to ya if I said no. Truth be told, when I was a young one my friends and I used to pick that back door lock right there and come in." He gestured to the door to the backyard located near the refrigerator. "We never did nothin' bad, we just would come in and pretend we were rich and sit by the fireplace. It sure is spooky at night."

"Well, yes. I can see that. It's a bright house in the day, but when night falls this place sure does look spooky. I'll give you that. Which is why I plan to install lights to light it up and make it brighter."

"It's a shame that this place has fallen into such disrepair. It woulda been majestic in its time. What are your plans? How can I help you?"

"I plan to restore it completely to its original splendor. We'll change out anything like bad plumbing, electric, et cetera, but I want to restore as much as possible back to its original look."

"That ain't gonna be cheap, Ma'am, you know that."

"I know it. But that's why I've got you here. You have a wonderful reputation of being honest and trustworthy. But you know I'm doing this as an investment, right? I intend to restore this so that I can flip it to a new owner, so I need stuff done well and fast."

John chuckled. "Ma'am, I'm 67 and been in the biz a long time. My boys have been subcontracting for me for years. I just need to know what and when and I'll have them snapping for ya fast."

Katie was skilled at renovating but had never taken on a project as big as this one. John kindly and patiently drew up a plan that would get the jobs done fast and efficiently, "without the boys being on top of one another."

"How soon can we start?" Katie asked.

"Well, I can do a full inspection right now and have a full quote to you by tomorrow night. My contractors are available for tomorrow if you want them to start working on fixin' and repairin' the outside. Might be able to have a couple boys here to do some interior dependin' on what I find with the inspection—"

"That's perfect! Let's do this, John," Katie said. She was anxious to just get going.

John grabbed his notepad and gulped down his coffee. In spite of his huge size and age, he was off in a flash. He seemed happy to be doing meaningful work, and Katie felt very comfortable around him. He felt a bit like a father figure.

Katie stood at the kitchen sink, looking out the window to the beautiful woods in the distance. A feeling of accomplishment overcame her, driven soul that she was. *This is going to be an awesome and profitable flip.* She was lost, daydreaming of the finished house, when John surprised her.

Nearly two hours had passed and John was ready to go. "Okay, the exterior guys will be here tomorrow at 7:00 AM. I'll see you tomorrow. Oh, and have a good night's sleep."

CHAPTER TWO

Katie returned home from town feeling jubilant. She had picked up a weekend's worth of groceries, six more bottles of red wine, and most importantly a dozen mousetraps.

After putting the food in the fridge she grabbed the bag of mousetraps and headed upstairs to the attic.

She pushed open the door and looked at the vast, empty space. The windows were dark, dusty and grimy but still let in enough light to see clearly. The attic had at one time been a room. Cleaned up it would be glorious again. *This would make a great granny suite*, Katie thought.

Unfortunately, the floor was completely covered with dust, dirt and rodent crap. Katie took out the 12 traps, loaded each one with a little bit of fresh bread and placed them all around the edges of the room. The room was in bad need of an airing out; it had dusty steel smell to it. Probably from the poop.

Katie was in bed by 10:00 PM. She was exhausted and was pleased to discover that she drifted off to sleep almost instantly. She woke up just after 2:00 AM to go for a pee. She paused and listened. The house was dead silent. Outside of the squeaking of the floorboards there was not a peep. Back to bed she went.

Scratch scratch. Scratch scratch scratch.

Katie's eyes popped open. "Too good to be true. I'll bide my time and I will get you, you little buggers," she said. She pulled the pillow over her head and rolled onto her right side, facing the window. It was a beautiful moonlit night. The men would be arriving early. She picked up her phone to check how much time she had left asleep. *Just over two hours.* It was 4:45 AM.

Katie was once again startled awake by what sounded like a freight train coming towards her. She sat bolt upright in bed. Diesel engines. Several. She reached over and grabbed her phone to look at the time. It was 6:55 AM.

"Oh my God. I forgot to set my alarm. They're here early. Crap!"

She scrambled out of bed, pulled on her jeans and sweater and tied her hair in a ponytail. She scrambled downstairs as four trucks pulled up outside of her house. By the time she got to the front door the men were unloading ladders, buckets and a variety of equipment.

"Good morning, miss!" shouted one of the gentlemen. He started walking towards her while barking out instructions to the guys. He walked up to Katie and extended his hand. "Hello, my name is Rick and I'm the foreman for today. We'll be doing some prep on your house. Are you familiar with what prep is—"

"Yes. I've been doing this for long time," Katie said. She laughed, as this wasn't her first time meeting a chauvinist. At least he was polite about it. "My name is Katie, and I'm the owner. If you need anything just give me a shout. Have fun!"

The men went to work unloading their equipment and setting up at the back of the house. The back of the house seemed to need the most work, so Katie was pleased they were starting there.

Katie decided that today would be the day she tackled the leaking toilet in the main bathroom. It wouldn't be the first time she'd replaced the seal on a toilet. It was a dirty job, but an easy one.

Before she headed up she decided to make a jug of iced green tea, her favorite thirst quencher. As she wandered into the kitchen it immediately felt darker. She glanced up at the light and it was working fine. She looked out the spacious windows and there wasn't a cloud in the sky. In fact it was a beautiful sunny day. And yet the kitchen seemed dark and heavy.

With the tea made and in her portable plastic jug she headed upstairs. Her toolbox was big and heavy. She was never afraid to spend money to get a job done, but liked to cut corners by doing as much as she could herself. Toilets were a specialty. Especially this one, as it was at least 50 years old and in great condition.

Time flew by and Katie heard the boys leaving, presumably for lunch. Her knees were sore from kneeling down on the tiled bathroom floor. What a feeling of accomplishment, though, as she had not only replaced the seal on the toilet but had also fixed the leaky faucets in the sink and the bathtub. As she stood up her stomach let out a loud growl. If the boys were going for lunch, she was gonna make herself lunch as well.

Katie headed down the creaky stairs and turned left into the kitchen. The kitchen smelled as though something had died in it. And it seemed even darker and gloomier than in the morning. She opened up the back door to let some fresh air in and immediately started investigating for a dead animal—rat, mouse, or whatever. She systematically went cupboard by cupboard but found nothing. Not even droppings.

She shrugged it off and made herself a fresh roast beef sandwich complete with fresh bread and a lovely helping of Dijon mustard. She almost inhaled the sandwich, she was so hungry. She debated about having another sandwich but decided otherwise as she was trying to keep her waistline from growing.

Perhaps it was the thought of a dead animal in her kitchen, but she cleaned the counters extra diligently just in case. "Cleanliness is close to godliness," she said to herself, thinking of her mother. She was falling in love with this kitchen. She loved the brightness, she loved the colors and she loved the space. *Maybe I should keep this house for myself?*

The back door slammed shut. Katie grabbed the counter and dropped her cloth. Her heart was beating a mile a minute. It scared the crap out of her. She was certain it was the wind, but she darted her eyes all around the kitchen just to make sure nobody—or no thing—had gotten in. *Damn wind scared the hell out of me.* She bent down, picked up the cloth and tossed it in the sink.

Katie was washing her hands when there was a knock at the front door. She grabbed the towel and headed for the door. It was Big John. Her heart was still racing when she got to the door.

"Hey John, how the heck are you?"

"I'm doing great, ma'am. Thanks for asking. I've got your full quote all worked out. Wanted to show to you." John said.

Katie noticed he was standing there kind of awkwardly and realized she should invite him in. A polite man. "That's awesome, come on in."

They headed into the kitchen where they had sat before and he opened up his binder. Katie asked him if he wanted anything and all he asked for was a glass of water. She poured the glass and sat down with him.

"Hey, guess what? I set enough mousetraps up in the attic to take out an army."

"Oh? Mousetraps? Those things aren't mice, it's a ghost! That's where one of the folks died—"

"What?"

"I'm just kiddin' ya. They are just—"

"Somebody died up there? What the hell?"

"Well..."

"Talk to me, Big John. Is that true?"

"Well... I'm surprised you didn't know that. An old woman was murdered up there eighty... maybe one hundred years ago..."

"Oh my God. Really? Are you kidding me or telling the truth?"

"Oh. It's the truth, ma'am. Wouldn't joke about that. Part of the problems you have with the house are from vandals: kids breaking in on dares, or to search for the ghosts. You name it. Place has sat empty for almost all of these years. Well, furnished and all, but empty as in nobody ever stays here long—"

"What happened?"

Big John let out a sigh and sat back in his chair. "Well, there are a few stories. But the one most agree on is that old John Blackstone lost his job and lost his mind. He murdered his wife and kids as well as his disabled Ma who lived in the apartment upstairs..."

"Good Lord."

"Weirdest part is that he completely vanished after—"

"Come on, John. You're just telling a ghost story."

"No, ma'am. He disappeared. Of course, it was easier to do that 80 years ago than today. But still, not a trace of him was found. They didn't discover the bodies for weeks. Everyone thought that they had taken a trip to see family. Pretty gruesome to say the least."

"Horrible—"

"But what you got upstairs ain't ghosts. They're roof rats. Pretty intelligent too. You gotta put the traps up there for a few days so they can mark them with their pee. Then you bait them. That's how you catch those guys. Ain't no other way—"

"They pee on them? That's interesting. So the traps are no good?"

"Total waste."

"Well, I guess I'll toss the traps and get some new ones."

John and Katie went over the proposal. It was broken into three parts: the exterior, interior and landscaping. Katie was extremely pleased, as he saw things that she had completely missed and his pricing was extremely fair. Big John lived up to his reputation of being honest to a fault. The only part that Katie declined was a section of the landscaping that she deemed unneeded. Didn't matter, it only shaved off a few dollars, but it made for a quicker turnaround.

With the exception of the landscapers—who were booked solid anyway—John guaranteed everything would be complete in less than five weeks, more likely four. This made Katie even happier.

Both agreed that almost everything was cosmetic, except a major rewiring job upstairs. Someone, at some time, had taken the trouble to rewire the downstairs but not the upstairs. Strange? Yes, but Katie had seen stranger.

Katie gave him a substantial deposit. More than she normally would, but she had an intuition that John would need it and it would help get things moving for both him and her.

Big John got up from the table and caught Katie off guard by giving her a sideways one-arm hug. "I'm gonna take care of you, little lady. You remind me of my daughter..." he said, his voice drifting off. It was comforting having such a large teddy bear of a man watching over her.

The boys were back at work as John headed out the front door. "Get to work, you lazy buggers!" he shouted, playfully, at the guys, to which they gave him 'yeah-yeah' nods and comments. Big John had a good crew assembled.

Katie rushed upstairs to get the sheets on the guest bed in anticipation of Mel coming. The bed, like hers, was brand spanking new in an original Queen Anne bedframe. The room looked beautiful. She was squealing with delight at the chance to spend time together.

Katie silently wished for an eventful weekend with Mel.

CHAPTER THREE

Katie didn't hear the car pull up, but she did hear the toot-toot of the car alarm and rushed downstairs. She could see Mel's black BMW parked out front. She got to the door just as the doorbell rang. She was excited.

"Hey, stranger!" Mel said. Mel had a loud voice that carried, and she was also excited to see her friend. They hugged in the doorway.

"Since this isn't your house, I got you a not-a-house-warming gift—"

"Come on, you didn't have to do that—"

"I brought six bottles of wine and a boatload of dark chocolates."

"We are going to be hung over this weekend, I can tell! I just picked up exactly six myself," Katie said.

"Well, the weekend is ticking away, let's get digging into a bottle!"

Katie grabbed Mel's bag and led her into the great room, which she called the library. It was a massive room with bookshelves all around with many books still there, some dating back to the 1920s. The main feature was a massive stone fireplace with a beautiful mantle and a giant painting of John Blackstone Sr., the original owner of the house. Katie had removed all of the sheets from the furniture, and although quite old, much of it was still nice and functional. It was like stepping back in time. The giant windows gave a view out of the front of the house to the beautiful trees of the forest down the hill.

Katie asked Mel to have a seat and get comfortable, but Mel was excited to see her and followed her into the kitchen. Katie placed the box with the six wine bottles on the counter and grabbed two wine glasses.

"I popped a bottle of Cabernet, so let's start with one of mine," said Katie.

"How are the guys working out for you?"

"Well, I'm using Big John, and his crew is doing fantastic. Fast workers. I'm happy."

"I envy you, Katie. I'd love to do what you do—the amazing transformations you do—but I'd probably kill all of the workers my patience is so short!"

Katie laughed. "You probably would. You do so well at real estate sales, I'm not sure why you'd want to get into this—"

"Money, baby. Money. This girl needs cash flow. How else can I afford cheap wine?"

"Hey, speaking of killing, why on earth didn't you tell me there was a murder here?"

"Never thought of it. Stories are all over the place with that, anyway. And it was a long time ago. Besides, I've never been in a haunted house before, and so I figured if you got it, I'd have my chance!"

"Sorry to disappoint, no ghosts here." Katie decided to leave out the information about the rats in the attic, then panicked, realizing that Mel would probably see them when she took her for a tour.

Katie chuckled to herself as her best friend chugged back the wine. "Tough day?"

"We had a legal problem with a house closing. Took hours to get resolved and was a royal pain. Need to drown it out with the wine tonight." Mel gave a fake laugh.

"Grab another glass, get settled into your room and I'll have supper ready shortly."

Katie took her upstairs to her room and Mel got settled in. Mel showered and changed into her 'comfies' consisting of an old grey pair of track pants, a t-shirt and a sweater. Katie made up a simple but delicious salad and roast chicken breast dinner. Wine flowed easily. After the meal, they retired back to the library.

"Let's start a fire," Mel said.

"Big John kind of discouraged me from setting fires."

"Why?"

"He said the chimney was in bad need of cleaning. He said if I started a fire not to let it go overnight."

"Come on. Let's just start a small one. I will make sure it's out before I go to bed."

Katie was nervous, but Mel knew a lot about houses and she trusted her. Besides, there was a damp chill in the library and a fire would probably get rid of that.

The women settled in with their wine and chocolates. There was a lot of laughter and fun in catching up.

"I love what you're doing with the bathroom upstairs, it looks great. My bedroom looks awesome, needs a little work but will be fantastic when done. I don't know what happened to the ceiling upstairs. Looks like a bomb hit it —"

"Yeah, the ceiling's been falling down. I've had to knock a few loose chunks off. But we'll get that fixed up as soon as the boys come back into the house."

"I love the fresh smell of lavender in the bathroom."

"Wait... You smelled the lavender too?" Katie was perplexed. "There were a couple days where the scent was overwhelmingly fresh, like a bouquet had been placed in the bathroom, but I can't figure out where it's coming from."

Mel paused. She wasn't sure if her friend was having fun and trying to spook her. "You don't have a can of air freshener or one of those scented stick thing-a-me-bobbers?"

"No." Katie was looking back at Mel and realized she was a bit skeptical. "Seriously. I've been working on that bathroom, cleaning the tiles, and I thought the same thing. I thought it was an air freshener. I checked everywhere. There's no way the scent would be that strong if it was just stuck to the wallpaper, do you think?"

"Well. The scent can certainly linger..." Mel realized her friend wasn't lying and wondered about it. "I'm going back up to see if the smell is still there."

Mel's sudden decision spooked Katie. The hairs stood up on her arms. Both women headed up the stairs to the second level. All the lights were on. *If Mel is trying to scare me, I'm gonna kill her*, Katie thought to herself.

Mel tilted her head back slightly and started sniffing. The sight made Katie giggle. But Mel was on a mission. She knew she didn't imagine it and was determined to find the source. The two wandered the upstairs, into the bathroom and even into the bedrooms. Nothing. If anything, the air was slightly stale.

After a few moments Mel made a pronouncement. "Beats me. I need more wine."

***

Katie opened her eyes. For a few moments she was unsure of where she was. Her neck was sore—she had a bad kink in it—and she rolled to her right side. She realized a number of things at once: she was in the great room, the fire was dying out, and she was lying on the couch with a pounding hangover headache.

Mel was gone. The nightlight in the kitchen was on, so she made her way upstairs. The other nightlight in the hallway was on too. She quietly tiptoed back to her room. Mel's door was wide open and she was lying face down on her bed, illuminated only by the moonlight. Katie could tell she had just taken her pants off, left her top on and dropped face down on the bed. As painful as her head was, she let out a little giggle and headed to bed herself.

CHAPTER FOUR

"Wow, my head hurts," Katie said to herself. She lifted her head from the pillow and looked down to see that she was fully clothed with the exception of bare feet.

Holy crap, what a hangover this is. She rolled over to her side, facing the window. Her head was pounding rhythmically but the silence brought her some peace. That is, the silence plus Mel's snoring next door. Otherwise, silence. Silence, pounding headache, and snoring. Great.

Katie's eyes started to close when she heard a weird noise outside. It was a dull thudding sound. Like someone was kicking a large bag of leaves across the backyard. It broke the silence because it was not rhythmic.

Katie got up and went to the window. The moon was bright and lit up the yard quite nicely. She couldn't see a thing.

Thud. Thud. Thud.

Well, I'm awake anyway. Let's see what this is.

Katie headed downstairs carrying one of her favorite secret weapons: a long metal police flashlight. The joke was that with the D batteries in the flashlight and the D cup boobs, she wasn't to be messed with!

Cautiously, Katie approached the front door, listening. There was a long pause, and she was about to head back upstairs when she heard another thud. She clicked the flashlight on and changed the setting to wide. She opened up the door slowly, shining light onto the front porch. It was all clear. Scanning the flashlight from the far left to the far right ever so slowly, she looked for any anomaly. There was none to be seen.

The thud happened again. Straight out in front of the house was a giant willow tree. It seemed that the thud was coming from there. A little nervous and yet brave at the same time, she slowly stepped out onto the porch. It was cold and damp to her bare feet.

She twisted the flashlight, changing the beam from wide to pinpoint. This was the setting her father had taught her to use when answering the door: the pinpoint would blind a troublemaker—and if necessary she could knock him out by smashing him over the head with the long handle.

Thud.

Curiosity just overcame her. The sound was not frightening in any way. At least that's what she told herself. Besides, the house was well lit on the outside, and with the moonlight she should be able to see anyone or anything coming out.

The grass was cool to her feet. And damp. But the night was still warm. With her head still pounding to the rhythm of her heart and the flashlight held at shoulder level she cautiously walked towards the willow. It was huge and majestic. Not scary at all. In fact, it felt like the tree was a protector. Sure, it had long, droopy branches, but the branches seemed to want to hug you, not hurt you.

As she drew closer she heard another thud. More like a thud and a rustling sound. She wondered if a bag of leaves was loose?

As comforting as the tree appeared, she didn't get too close. She stood about 10 feet away from the trunk and slowly walked around. Nothing.

Katie looked back at the house. In the darkness you couldn't see its blemishes, and with the moonlight and the lights it looked brand-new.

All of the windows had a yellow-orange glow to them. Her imagination took her back to the turn of the century, when houses would be lit by candlelight or lanterns. The upstairs was lit brighter than downstairs. Mel's room—the guest room—was glowing brighter than all the rest.

Katie was shaken from her daydream by the sound of a loud scream. A scream of absolute terror. Katie's body tightened up and she raised the flashlight above her head as her heart pounded. She was absolutely frozen. Her feet seemed stuck to the grass. Another scream. She looked towards Mel's room and saw a shadow flicker past the window.

Mmmmmm. Mmmmmmmmm! Katie tried to scream Mel's name out but she could not. The lights of the house seemed to dim as Mel's room got brighter. Katie's chest felt like it was going to explode her heart was pounding so quickly. She was gritting her teeth but not a word could come out. She tried to move her legs—to run—not away, but to the house. She could not. She was paralyzed in utter fear.

MMMMMMmmmmm. Katie still couldn't speak, but she felt a surge of adrenaline run through her body. She leaned forward to race towards the house but someone grabbed her left arm at the wrist to hold her back. It was cold and it hurt.

Katie turned quickly to her left with her flashlight swinging through the air, intending to hit whomever—or whatever—was holding her back from saving her friend's life. From right to left the flashlight swung, cutting only through the air. She turned the flashlight downwards to see what was holding her left wrist.

From out of the ground a branch or a root had attached itself to her wrist. The root was alive, and like an octopus's tentacles it continued to wrap itself around her wrist and started moving up towards her elbow.

Katie was filled with a blend of horror and anger. She didn't stop to wonder how this was happening. She only cared about her friend in the house. With all her might she raised the flashlight up and smashed it down on the branch or root. At the moment of impact the willow tree seemed to shudder and she heard the sound of the leaves. The same sound that she had heard from the house.

Viciously she struck and struck the branch. The more she hit it the more rustling she heard, but she quickly discovered it was futile: It was growing thicker and grabbing her left arm harder, and it was moving up quickly to her shoulder. It was as if every single strike—every single effort—held her back more. She twisted towards the house.

"Mel!" Katie screamed. Her eyes were bulging.

"No. No, no, no!" she heard screamed from within the house.

Mel's light suddenly went off. Another scream. This time different. This was a scream of pain. Anguish.

The lights in the house suddenly shut off as though being killed by a master switch.

Katie had never felt this level of fear in her whole life. Her heart was pounding a mile a minute. The screams stopped. Mel didn't answer. Was she okay? Was she still alive?

One thing was for sure. Her arm was becoming extremely sore and whatever the hell this was that was holding her back needed to be killed really fast.

Katie turned back towards the tree and the branch protruding from the ground with its tentacles all wrapped around her left arm. Whatever this was, Katie's only thought was that it had picked the wrong day to screw with her.

Again Katie took the flashlight and started smashing the branch. She smashed it over and over again, turning her focus and energy towards a one-inch spot. It seemed to be working, as the bark chipped off and she could smell the fresh green vine as she continued to whack it.

In the heat of the moment Katie marveled at her ability to channel fear into desperation. Her friend was in trouble, and whatever this was would be eliminated in short order.

A strange thing occurred. As she brought down the flashlight she seemed to strike a nerve in the branch. A massive whack and the branch seemed to pull back, yanking her to the ground. She landed face down, the left side of her face pounding the ground. It stunned her for second and hurt like hell.

The flashlight, still glowing, lay about three feet away from her, shining on her face. Her head hurt, her arm hurt, and a bright light beamed in her eyes. She felt like she was about to pass out. Sheer terror enveloped her.

She slammed her right hand down and lifted up her head, only to discover she was staring at her wall.

Her head was pounding, her heart was beating faster than it ever had before, and her left arm was folded under her body on the bed.

Katie flipped over and sat upright in bed. Her left arm was absolutely numb with pins and needles from being 'asleep.'

A nightmare. She got up, rushed to the window and looked out. Silence. No funny sounds. Nothing but a pounding headache, silence, and the sound of someone sleeping next door. Snoring. Mel.

Katie ran her right hand over her left arm a number of times to try to get the blood back. It had seemed so real. She looked down the hallway, lit only by a nightlight. The stairs were faintly lit, just barely, by the nightlight from the kitchen.

"I gotta cut back on the drinking," Katie said to herself.

Katie looked back at the willow tree. There it stood in the moonlight. It was large and looming. She glared at it for hurting her. *I'll cut your ass down. I'll fix you*, she thought.

She continued to stare at it. It didn't seem particularly threatened by her mental taunt. Most inanimate objects don't fret over such things, after all.

Katie took off her pants and bra and bounced back into bed. It took her a while, but she eventually fell asleep.

CHAPTER FIVE

"Oh my God!"

Katie jumped to her feet, grabbed her jeans and tugged them on as quickly as possible. It was eight in the morning and the sound from the diesel trucks woke her up. The boys were back to continue work on the outside. They were already stepping out of the trucks and her pants weren't even halfway up.

She waddled down the hallway to the guest room only to see Mel still lying in virtually the same position, face down on the bed butt-naked from the waist down. Her curtains were wide open. Right where the boys were to be working. Katie ran into her room, reached down and slapped her on her right butt cheek. Whack.

Simultaneously as Mel jumped startled to her feet, Katie ran to the curtains and swished them shut.

"What the hell? What the... Oh my God, my head hurts," Mel said. She was half awake, stumbling for words.

"The boys are here. I didn't want them staring at your big ass," Katie said. She giggled.

"Dear God. That's disgusting," Mel said, looking down. She pulled her shirt down to cover her crotch area.

Katie giggled as she skirted out the door, leaving Mel to get dressed. She hustled downstairs and into the kitchen.

Katie stopped dead in her tracks.

All the papers, everything that had been on the kitchen table, was now scattered all over the floor. A number of things from the kitchen countertop were also on the floor, including tea packages, flyers and mail. It looked like someone had ransacked the kitchen. A burglar?

Katie jumped towards the top drawer at the far left of the kitchen counter, where she kept her flashlight to use for protection. She yanked open the drawer and discovered it was missing.

She felt her chest tighten with fear. Was an intruder still in the house? She jumped to the side door: It was locked. Kitchen windows, locked. She cautiously walked into the great room and everything seemed in order.

There was a knock on the front door. She scurried over and opened it quickly, knowing that there would be a worker there. The door was locked.

"Hello, miss. Good morning to you. Is it all right if we get working on the house now?" the young man asked.

"Yes... Yes, sure. Thanks for coming," she said.

The young man gave her a quizzical look. "Did you forget we were coming, miss?" He smiled.

Katie let out a fake laugh. "Yes, yes I did. Thanks for coming," she said. She smiled awkwardly as she caught the man drop his eyes quickly to her boobs before dragging them back to her face as she closed the door.

Nice! Mel thought.

Katie swung around, startled. She hadn't heard Mel come down the stairs.

Mel was comically popping her eyeballs out, staring at Katie's breasts. "Nice headlights! Giving the guy an incentive for the day, are you?"

"Shut up," Katie said. She folded her arms across her boobs and headed to the kitchen.

"What the hell happened here?" Mel said.

"That's what I'd like to know. How much did we have to drink last night?"

"Four bottles, and a fifth one uncorked... looks untouched," Mel said, looking at one of the bottles. "That was a rough one. I don't remember going to bed."

"Well, you left me on the couch downstairs. Thanks a lot," Katie said. She was teasing, of course.

"Oh yeah? I woke up in a strange bed without any pants and no man beside me. I think I got the worst end of the deal," Mel said. Both ladies laughed.

Katie confessed, "I thought someone might have broken into the house." She gave a weak laugh. "I guess one of us must have knocked the stuff off—"

"Maybe it's the rats?"

"Don't think so. No poop in the kitchen, or markings. Doubt it."

"Ghosts!" Mel held out her hands. "Whoooooooohhhh-hh..."

Both women giggled and Mel announced she was going to brush her teeth and get into some work clothes. Katie got out some cereal boxes, milk, bowls and spoons. And coffee. *Can't ever start a day without coffee.*

***

"Hey, check this out—"

"Jeepers! Did you go to ninja training school or something?" Katie said. Clearly, she had the jitters.

"Sorry. Seriously, check this out." Mel held out her hand with something shiny in it. It was a heart-shaped locket, silver with ornate detail. The locket was almost black with tarnish.

Katie took it in her hand and turned it over. It had two initials inscribed on it: A.B.

"B would be from Blackstone, I would think. I wonder who the A was for?"

"That's not the weird part. You won't believe where I found it," Mel said. She waved her hand for Katie to follow her as she burst up the stairs.

Katie was right behind her and they both entered Mel's guestroom together.

"Look on the floor over there. Look at the scratches on the old wallpaper just above the baseboard," Mel said.

"Okay. I don't see anything."

"Look along the bottom edge of the baseboard. Just run your eye from left to right and tell me what you see," Mel said.

"Okay. I see floor, baseboard, wall..." Katie's voice drifted off and she squinted. She saw something dark, like a pencil or pen shoved underneath the baseboard between it and the floor. Actually, it looked more like it was jammed under there.

"You see?" Mel said.

Katie said nothing. She walked towards the baseboard and dropped down to her hands and knees to take a better look. "What is it?"

"You'll figure it out. If I can figure it out you will."

"Weird, it looks like a... hinge."

"Look at the scratches and where they are... Use your imagination, girl!"

Katie had no idea what she was doing, but she instinctively put her fingers on the top edge of the baseboard where the scratches were. She gave the baseboard an ever-so-gentle tug but nothing happened.

"I'll save you time. I did exactly the same thing. Pull harder!"

Katie dug her fingers in a little deeper and pulled towards herself. The baseboard dropped down with a snap and Katie jumped backwards a bit. The baseboard had opened up to reveal a hidden hole in the wall. The hole was rectangular and dark as the night. Katie was a bit jittery about this and slid back some.

"It was right there."

"You actually reached in there?"

"More like snatched it out of there. We should get a flashlight and check it out. I wonder why someone would have a secret spot like that?"

"I have a big-ass flashlight downstairs in the kitchen... Actually... I don't know where it is."

"You only have one flashlight?"

"Actually I do have another, but it's in a box somewhere. But the guys that are here, if they've got one we could borrow it."

The women both headed downstairs and exited through the back door in the kitchen. Before Katie could say anything Mel eyeballed the young guy on a ladder closest to the kitchen window. "We lost our flashlight. Do you have one, and if so can we borrow it?"

The young man stopped scraping the paint and turned towards the two ladies. His very first expression seemed to be one of annoyance, but that changed when he saw two women standing below him. His demeanor quickly changed. Covered completely in dust and paint, he tried to be as gentlemanly as possible.

"Sure, ladies. Let me grab one from my truck."

Mel and Katie looked at each other. Katie knew exactly what Mel was thinking: Here's a hot guy doing her bidding.

"Did he say he wanted to grab me and f—"

"You are worse than a guy. Sex, sex, sex. That's all you think about," Katie said. She winked at Mel. "He does have a nice ass."

Both ladies laughed. The young man hurried back with an extra-large yellow flashlight. It was well worn, beaten and abused.

"We'll bring it right back. Thanks very much," Mel said. Her voice had dropped slightly, in a slightly seductive way.

As the ladies hurried back into the house, Katie said, "You are such a tease! The poor boy won't be able to sleep tonight."

"Well, there's room in my bed," Mel said. She giggled.

"Not in my holy house, you filthy wench."

The women laughed like schoolgirls as they headed into Mel's room. They both dropped to the floor, turning on the flashlight and directing it so they could peek in the hole.

The secret hiding space was about a foot wide and two feet deep. It was about three inches high. A spot big enough to hide documents, important papers, or jewelry.

Sure enough, there was something in the far back.

"Grab it," said Katie.

"YOU grab it."

They both laughed. The girls looked at each other, neither one having the guts to do it.

"What if it's a rat?" said Mel.

"It would probably stink to high heaven."

Katie leaned down and looked again. "I'm going for it."

Mel moved back in anticipation of something jumping out. "If it gets you, I can be a witness and not a victim," she said, teasing.

"Stop it. I'm scared enough."

"But I got the necklace. Your turn," said Mel.

Katie positioned herself so she could slide her right arm in quickly, grab whatever it was, and then pull it out fast. She looked at Mel for encouragement.

"For God's sake, just do it!"

Katie thrust her hand in and snatched the thing out quickly, dropping it right by the opening. She jumped up and danced around. "Jeez, that gave me the heebie-jee-bies!"

"What is it?" Mel asked.

Lying on the floor was an old weathered leather file holder. It was wrapped with a red string and extremely dusty. It had an old musty smell.

Katie untied the bow and opened it. The papers inside were yellowed and the writing appeared to be ink from an elegant fountain pen.

"It's a ledger," said Mel. "Clearly a secret one."

Katie peered into the opening with the flashlight. It was now empty.

"Wonder if there are any other secret spots?" Mel said.

Both women jumped to their feet and hurried into the master bedroom. Instinctively they split in two directions,

Katie taking one side and Mel taking the other. There was no such trap or hidden spot to be found.

They headed to the second bedroom. It had not been touched in any way, shape or form since Katie had purchased it. The floor in the room was covered in dust. But that didn't stop them. They checked the floorboards but found nothing.

"God, this room smells like... death," Mel said in a low voice. Her nose was wrinkled in disgust.

"Hey, that's what you are here for, to help me bring this back to life!"

They stepped out into the hallway. Mel started to head up the stairs to the attic, but Katie stopped her. "Rats," she said.

Mel shuddered. "I hate rats... why don't you get a team of exterminators to nuke them?"

"I've already got Big John—"

"And you never told me? Some friend YOU are!" Mel said indignantly. She was only half-joking. Rats scared the life out of her. "I'm starving, what's for breakfast?"

The two women headed back to the kitchen. Katie had already eaten, so Mel poured a bowl of corn flakes and headed to the library. She plopped onto a very comfortable Queen Anne chair and started eating. Katie followed behind with a fresh coffee.

"I'll ask Mr. Watkin about the locket when I see him next," Katie said.

"That boy creeps me out," Mel said.

"Tell me about him. Why exactly did he want to sell this place? How did it get so run down?"

"Well, you know, there's all kinds of rumors and it's hard to separate fact from fiction. All I can tell you is what I heard..."

"Just start me from the beginning," Katie said, nudging her friend along. Mel had a bad habit of going all over the place with her stories. Getting her focused could be tricky at times.

"Believe it or not, he was apparently a good looking young man many years ago. A drummer in a band, I think. Not professional, but they played around town. He met a woman named Petula Blackstone and they got married.

"Word had it that she was wealthy. Some say she wasn't. I think she had cash but was very frugal. They stretched out their dollars, know what I mean?"

Katie nodded. Mel was a good story teller, and her eyes were focused on the fireplace mantle as she spoke.

"So... they have a kid. A girl. A pretty thing—I've seen old pictures—and they are living the American dream. Mom is at home, kid is in school and Chris is working at a pen factory, I think. Something to do with pens, anyway.

"One day the daughter dies. Killed in a car wreck. No drugs. No alcohol. Just one of those tragic things that happen.

"Good God. How awful!" Katie said.

"Tell me about it. That would mess you up, for sure. And apparently it did. Mom became a recluse in her home. She used to attend church regularly, the whole nine yards.

"Messed up Chris too. He continued to show up to work and around town getting groceries and stuff, but everyone said he became a ghost. His old band got together for some reunion and they tried to get him to play but he ignored them. Poor guy."

"But that wouldn't creep people out," Katie said. "That's just tragic, not creep-factor stuff—"

"Oh, just wait. I'm getting to the creep now," Mel said. She was leaning forward on her chair, and lowered her voice. "Here's where the weird stuff starts happening."

Katie leaned in to listen.

"Petula had a fall here at the house. Depending on who you talk to, it was outside or inside. All I know was it was stairs. Broke her hip badly, was in the hospital for a short time and then back here to recover.

"Chris was even more distraught and did everything he could to make her comfortable. She refused nurses coming to see her and doctors from following up. She was a miserable woman from what everyone says. Stubborn.

"He goes to the effort of putting a bed in here—the library—because she can't do stairs. You know, close to the kitchen and that bathroom around the corner. She doesn't like it one bit and is making life miserable for everyone, including Chris. She needs to be supervised for everything, that's how bad her hip was.

"So, one day Chris is out in the front yard. He sees a light on upstairs, which is weird, so he goes to check..." Mel paused to take a sip of her coffee.

"Go on, for God's sake. Don't leave me hanging!" Katie said, slightly irritated.

"Petula isn't in her bed. She's not in the kitchen. He hears water running. She somehow managed to get upstairs and was trying to take a bath—"

"He heard the water running?"

"Yes, it's running and he's upset. She's supposed to get help with stuff like that. So, he runs upstairs angry and knocks on the door. It's closed, obviously, but she doesn't answer. He opens the door and finds her... dead... with the water running—"

"Dead? IN the tub or—"

"IN the tub. Apparently she was getting in, slipped and fell backward. Banged her head against the wall and drowned—"

"Oh my God! That's horrible."

"No. That's not the worst of it. Police do an investigation and for a short time Chris was a suspect in her death."

"Wha... huh? Why? I don't get that—"

"Well, the autopsy initially said she drowned-and she did-but the blow to the head was ultimately what killed her. It took a while, but they proved somehow that she died by accident."

"Can you imagine? Being accused of killing your spouse? Jeez. Your wife dies tragically and then you are suspected of killing her? That's pathetic."

"Yeah, the police took a beating over that too. The Sheriff resigned not long after. He sucked."

"I'm guessing Chris felt guilty over it, even though it wasn't his fault. He lived here for several years, but rumors spread of his strange behavior.

"A guy I know, David, used to deliver the paper to him. When he'd collect the cash... gosh... this is going wayyyy back... they don't do that anymore... remember the tabs and how they used to collect..."

"Focus, Mel, focus," Katie said. She was irritated.

"David would come to the door and he says that all the furniture was covered in white cloths. Didn't like coming too late as he was spooked out by the house at night. Only a bedroom light would be on and maybe the kitchen light. Freaky."

Katie let it sink in for a moment. "I'll say. But then again, maybe he just couldn't bear to be in the library where her bed was."

"True enough. But what would be horrible for me is to use the bathroom she died in. I couldn't do it," Mel said. "But you've got to expect a house that's this old would have a number of tragedies or deaths over the years, they all do at some point, or—"

"Stop. What? How many deaths are we talking about here?" Katie's voice was hollow. She felt like she was the last person in the United States to be learning something about the house.

Mel paused awkwardly. "Well, as I said, old homes, you know, have a lot of history to—"

"Just need a number, Mel. One, two... how many?"

Mel shifted in her chair and blurted out, "Five. Maybe six."

Katie sat stunned for a moment, but flashed back to her history class in school. She recalled how most people used to die at home. Viewings would take place in the front room. That's not so bad, she thought to herself. She wasn't prepared for what Mel said next.

"Murdered. Late 1800s. Blackstone wiped out his whole family and just up and disappeared. Some think that—"

"Slow the hell down! Murdered... here? In THIS house?"

Mel's face was blank. She felt a bit bad that her best friend was getting upset about it, but she needed to hear it. It was about to get worse.

"Where did the murders take place?" Katie demanded. She got up and paced for a few seconds and then walked into the kitchen to get the coffee pot.

"Um. Well. I don't know for sure, but I understand he murdered all his family in various parts of the house and piled them—"

"Piled them? Jesus! How much worse can this get? And why the hell didn't you tell me about this?" Katie was getting pretty upset.

"Calm down, chickie. First, you're not going to be living here, this is a flipper. The rumors of it being haunted aren't being helped by the fact it looks like a haunted house. These guys are going to have the outside sparkling in no time and it'll sell."

Katie paused. Mel was right. Sober up, have some more caffeine and get focused. "What do you mean, piled up?" she asked calmly.

"Well, we know he killed them all one by one. We know that he stacked them neatly in the library—"

"Stacked them?"

"Well, I don't know. Probably lined them up. Here. In the library."

"What happened to him?"

"That's the strange part. He vanished. Not a single trace was ever found of him. No sightings, nothing. Money left in the bank, belongings mostly intact. Some suspect he killed himself in the forest behind here, but his body has never been found."

"Who were the family members?"

"He shot his wife in the kitchen, killed his three kids and then his mother who lived in the attic, which was converted to a bedroom."

"Good God. So that's..." Katie was counting on her fingers, "six deaths that we know of in this house."

"Yep. And you wonder why kids would break in to stay in the haunted house?" Mel asked.

CHAPTER SIX

"Bad news and good news," Mel said. She was carrying her bag and put it down in the living room.

"Oh?"

"I need to go into the office to sign the legal paperwork for that multi-house transaction. It's messy as hell and I got to be there. The good news is it'll only take a few minutes to do and the lawyers are waiting for me."

"Well that's a bummer." Katie looked genuinely down and upset by this.

"You are way too stressed out. You are hardly getting any sleep, you're pushing yourself way too hard, and you're imagining things—"

"Imagining things? What's that supposed to mean?"

"See what I mean?" Mel said, with her hands on her hips.

"Sorry. But I'm not imagining things. Weird stuff is happening here. This place has a bizarre vibe to it."

"Whatever. Come back to my place and hang out for the day. We'll go out for a nice dinner tonight. You come back to my place, crash, get a good night's sleep, and head home in the morning."

"Well..."

"Screw the 'well.' Just say yes, get your stuff and let's get going. I gotta run."

"But what about the boys?"

"What about them? They've got their jobs to do, you can leave the key under the mat, and there's nothing in this house for them to steal that couldn't have been stolen over the past 50 years!"

Katie paused, and then burst out laughing. "You do have a point."

"Get your ass upstairs, get packed and let's get going. The lawyers are waiting for me. Call Big John and tell him that the key is under the front mat."

***

"We're just gonna stop in to the office for a few minutes, if that's cool with you. Signing the paperwork will only take a few moments to do, then we can go back to my place and crash. Is that cool with you?" Mel said.

"Sounds great to me," Katie said. She was running her hand along the edge of the black leather seat of Katie's Mercedes. She called it the 'big-ass black Merck.'

"God, I love your car, Mel."

"Well, it's not my car. The bank lets me use it for very generous monthly payments," she laughed. "When you own a real estate business you have to look the part of success, dress the part of success, and have the bank loans to create the illusion."

"You can't fool me. You are successful, in spite of the loans. You're doing fantastic, so don't try to BS me in any way, shape or form. I'll smack you."

"Well, I have done well for myself, I have to say. After a long line of losers in my family I'm the first to succeed."

It was a sad comment to make, but unfortunately it was true. Mel's mother had died from substance abuse, and she had an absent father who did transient jobs. She had started work when she was young, doing odd jobs just to be able to afford a pair of jeans.

Mel had always been good-looking, and a bit of a rebel. When she was 16 she was dating a 24-year-old man who was into real estate. He was a hustler—in a good way —working long hours day after day. He focused on getting listings instead of easy sales and ended up making a small fortune, buying a Porsche with cash. They split up, but she got her real estate license and her inspired drive from him.

Hadn't taken long for Mel to realize she could make more money owning a real estate firm with people working for her and having her signs all over town: Wragg-Brattle Real Estate.

Katie was proud of her best friend.

Mel's house was ranch style and ridiculously huge at 7,500 square feet. Mel claimed she 'needed' it for parties and events. It was in an upper class area, which Mel loved. It validated her.

Mel popped a bottle of wine and brought Katie a glass in the massive living room. Katie sat in possibly the world's most comfortable leather recliner with what seemed like a bazillion different comfort settings. She fiddled with the buttons.

Legs too high. Okay, too low. What the hell is poking my back? Ooops. Ohhh. That is perfect...

Mel headed to her home office—much bigger than her office in town—to take care of some loose business ends. Katie sipped her wine while enjoying the view of the woods and the small lake down the hill.

This is awesome. Just awesome. I needed this, she thought. She reached down into her leather bag, pulled out her laptop, flipped open the screen and pressed the power button.

"Hey, Mel! What's the Wi-Fi password?"

"Naked men wanted one two three—all one word and lowercase..."

"Pig!"

"Complain when those Australian studs drop by for a drink tonight..."

Katie giggled and shook her head. She began a search online for old newspaper archives. After several false starts she signed up for one that offered unlimited searches for seven days for free.

She typed in 'Blackstone Manor + murders.' A cute miniature newspaper popped up and spun around in circles for what seemed like ages. As she was sipping her wine and anticipating a tough search she was surprised to find that 13 hits appeared.

The first headline said "Family Massacred, Father Wanted" and she immediately clicked.

[Story]

November 8, 1954, Riverside: Police report of a grisly discovery of five bodies at the Blackstone Manor off of Main Street. Sheriff is refusing to release other details at this time, other than to say that there was an attempted arson as well. Police are seeking John Blackstone, who is missing. Bodies were discovered by a 13-year-old boy who called on the Blackstone residence to visit a friend. The town is in shock.

Mel broke Katie's concentration when she appeared with the bottle of wine. "How are you doing, need some more?"

Katie replied no, but discovered her glass was empty. "Well, maybe another glass. Hey, I found the newspaper report of the murders at my house—"

"What? How? Online? You can do that?"

"Yeah, I just found a newspaper morgue online. Just like a search engine, you type in something and it pulls up results. The murders made the news all across the States."

"What's it tell you?"

"Hang on, I just read the first one. Doesn't tell us anything much, other than it happened in November 1954."

"That's weird, I thought the murders were in the 1920s. Still, a long time ago... hey, what else does it say?"

Mel poured a glass for each of them and settled into the matching recliner. She pressed a button and was instantly comfortable. Her chair seemed a mile away from Katie.

"Still checking. Nothing we don't know already, except a kid found the bodies..."

"Oh God. How horrible. Does it say a name?"

"No. I'm just at the breaking news... God, I'm glad times have changed, there's an article about people trying to get rid of blacks from town..."

"You said the 50s, pretty sad time for racism."

"Oh my God..."

"What? What are you reading?"

"The next day they revealed it was five family members. The wife, three kids and mother. All were shot all through the house. Appears that the middle child put up a struggle..." Katie was trying to read and talk at the same time.

"Don't leave me hanging!"

"The boy's name was Daniel. Police figure he was trying to save his sister and was shot doing so. It goes on to say that the mother was shot upstairs in her room and it appears that she was dragged partway but left in the doorway." Katie let out another half-laugh.

"What."

"Again, different times. Described the mother as being quite fat. Nice."

"Agree. Glad times have changed. Hey, what about the fire, any mention of that?

Katie was distracted. "Nah... wait... duplicate story... oh, it looks like someone tried to start a fire but it didn't catch. Although it does say the police were amazed as there were gas cans and rags. 'Miracle' is the word describing it."

Katie kept clicking different newspaper stories. Some were from different newspapers but were duplicates. "Here's another: John Blackstone wanted for the murders of his family. Absolutely no trace of him, although it is confirmed he withdrew $9,000.00 from his mother's bank account—"

"That would have been a ton of cash back then. And it would have been cash. How the heck do you—"

"Oh my God..."

"Don't do that! Spit it out," Mel said.

"Oh my. God."

"Did you hear what I just—"

"Jesus. The thirteen-year-old boy who found the family was Chris Watkin—"

"WHAT?"

"Apparently found the bodies and witnessed John Blackstone leave the house—"

"Where did he go?"

"It just says Watkin mentioned the forest. A police search turned up nothing, but the Sheriff at least admitted that they didn't search till the next day—"

"And if you think our police department is small now, it was just a few people back then. This is a pretty quiet town."

Katie glanced out the floor-to-ceiling windows at the lake below. "That would mess anyone up. For sure. Poor kid. Good grief, I should say poor man..."

Mel joined Katie in staring out the window. "Did they ever find this bastard?" Katie asked out loud. She began searching the laptop again.

"Not a trace, according to stories I've heard. They checked bus stations, train stations, airports, everything. If he did skip town, he did it cleanly.

"How does anyone disappear?"

"Again, chickie, different times. Rumor has it he moved to a new town, took up a new identity and that was that."

Katie was reading as they talked. "Crazy..."

Mel waited. Nothing. "You are doing it again. Crazy... WHAT?"

"2004 was the fiftieth anniversary of the massacre, and they used the fingerprints from John Blackstone to do a search in the crime database. In 2014 they did it again with a DNA sample, but it didn't work..." Katie said.

"You know what creeps me out? He could be in a town murdering people and getting away with it—"

"Here's an article that says the family was extremely religious and fanatics—"

"Actually, I don't think that's true. Apparently the whole family stopped going to church. Blackstone taught Sunday school and kept going. If anyone was a fanatic, it was probably him. Don't think the family was."

Katie was excited. She kept interrupting with 'updates' that she was reading. Mel didn't mind, as it was clearing up the story and separating fact from fiction.

"Oh. Here's another one. Two weeks before the murders he was fired from the sawmill. Company was bought out and they eliminated a bunch of management jobs and laid off a number of workers. He was a casualty. Witnesses say he showed up at the library daily in his business suit and read books all day long, as in he was trying to keep it secret."

"Freaky," Mel said.

"Shizzah!"

"I'm going to smack you..."

"Dear Lord."

"Okay," Mel said, pressing the buttons to make her chair return to the sitting position, "I'm coming over and I'm gonna slap you out..."

Katie turned and laughed. "Sorry. It's just incredible what you can find online. There's an article about Christopher Watkin and the weird death of his wife. It references that she's from the Blackstone lineage and how weird it is that he married into the family after their deaths —"

"Oh, it's weird alright. But when you know the backstory it makes sense—"

"Whatever, but doesn't it seem weird he witnesses the deaths, then marries the niece, who then dies and suddenly he owns everything? Mentions he became a millionaire.

No mention of his background other than 'humble"
family."

"So. The story goes that the Blackstone family felt sorry for him and would console him by having him over for
Christmas dinner, New Year's, etc. And it became a tradi-
tion. He and Martha fell in love and got married young."

"The house... it was cleaned up and given to the young
couple. Which is friggin' weird if you ask me. Can you
imagine? Saying, 'Sweetie, you know the house your aunt
was massacred in and your new husband witnessed it?
Yeah... it's all yours now!'"

"Ugh. Horrible. Never thought of that! What kind of a
monster would do THAT?" Katie twisted her face in disgust. She shifted in her chair just thinking about it.

"Yeah, weird as hell—"

"Oh my God—"

"Not again!" Mel said.

Katie had put the laptop on the coffee table and was
holding her glass of wine. She was frozen. Mel leaned in.
Katie was processing something in her head, finding
words to describe what appeared to be a horrible thought.

"Uh. Yesterday... I was in the library and I thought I
saw a worker near the willow tree. I did a double-take and
noticed Chris Watkin just... standing... by the tree—"

"What was he doing? How come you didn't tell me?"

"...Well, he wasn't doing anything. He actually was
resting his back against it and just... looking at the
house..."

"And..."

"Well, I went out to see him. He just said he wanted to see how the house was coming along and commented on how beautiful the outside was looking. Seemed harmless enough..."

"And..."

"Well, now that I think of it, I don't recall seeing a car and don't recall hearing a car pull up."

"He actually gets around on a scooter. Perfect, as he's a weird looking guy on a weird looking yellow scooter—"

"Uh-huh. But I've been getting a feeling of being watched. At first I thought squatters, maybe a peeping Tom... you don't think it would be him, do you?"

"As weird as he is, I don't think so. His scooter does about 10 MPH and it's a long way to come across town... he had the place all these years, I think it's natural for him to come and see it. Promise me you'll tell me if he shows up again?"

"I will."

CHAPTER SEVEN

Where am I? was Katie's first waking thought. She found herself lying in a king bed in a mostly white decorated room. She blinked her eyes and realized she was at Mel's house. She could smell coffee.

Tossing off the duvet, she opened the silk curtains, exposing a stunning morning view of the forest and the lake below. There was a dock, but no boat. Mel had talked about getting a houseboat to go cruising, but it would have to wait till next year.

Katie opened her door and headed to the kitchen. She was expecting to find Mel, but found a note by the coffee maker: "Hey, fresh coffee for you. When you leave, please text me and I'll set alarm. Fun times. Love ya. M"

Katie poured a coffee and headed to the living room to enjoy the cup and view.

Last night had been a relaxed and enjoyable night in town with a great friend and fabulous Italian food.

Katie sat her coffee cup down and went to pick up her laptop from the coffee table. On top of the laptop was a business card: 'Psychic Diana—Crystal and Tarot reader, house blessings a specialty.'

Katie let out a laugh. She had laughed last night too when Mel suggested getting this woman to come and 'bless' the house with sage to cast out any unwanted spirits or energy. She was shaking her head when her cell phone rang.

"Oh my God, Big John. I forgot to tell you I'd be out!"

"Well, it's kinda hard to install stuff in yer house if you aren't around to open the door." He laughed, but it was a polite laugh. As in: I'm laughing, but it's not funny, you idiot.

"So sorry. The key is under the mat at the door..." she paused, and could hear him grunting as he was bending down.

"Found it. Is it okay for me to go in and install the alarms?"

"Please do. Sorry. I'll be back soon."

Katie hung up the phone. She fired up her laptop, answered a few emails and made a short list of groceries, a few items needed for the house, and not long after headed out.

"How the heck am I going to get home without a car?" she said out loud. For a woman who planned down to the tiniest detail, she couldn't believe how scatterbrained she felt.

At the same time, she felt more relaxed than ever before. Everything was going smoothly now, the main work outside was amazing and the 'boys' would have the inside done shortly. She envisioned another nice, profitable flip.

***

"We'll take the back route, there's construction up ahead, miss," said Eddie, the non-stop gabbing taxi driver.

They drove off of the main street through a residential area. Katie was daydreaming and basking in the wonderful relaxed feeling she felt. She'd have to thank Mel for that when they spoke next.

As the cab made its way down the street she saw a sign outside of one particularly large house with beautiful wooden siding that said "Dentist."

A bit further along was another sign. Not so nice. A bit gaudy looking, with Christmas lights on it. As they drove closer she couldn't believe her eyes.

"Eddie. Did Mel set you up to take me this way?"

Eddie flinched. "No, ma'am. The road is blocked. It would have been much faster had it not been blocked. This is the next fastest way. Why?"

"Nothing," Katie said. She thumped back against the seat and gazed out as they passed by the home of Psychic Diana.

"Psychic Diana. Does she wear a turban and robes?"

Eddie laughed out loud. "No, actually, she dresses in normal clothes and is a nice lady. Raises a lot of money for charity, especially the school. She's pretty normal."

Katie let out a 'hmph' as the cab struggled to get up the steep drive to the house. Eddie was still gabbing away: "Can you imagine back in the late 1800s a horse having to pull a wagon up here? It must have darn near killed the horses..."

Katie tuned him out. As they turned the corner she saw ladders all over the place, a pickup truck loaded with junk and garbage and at least a dozen men walking around. She was impressed.

"Thanks for the ride, Eddie," she said. "Keep the change."

She turned to walk away and Eddie piped up, "Hey, do you like Italian food? I know a great place I'd love to show you..."

Katie blushed. Awkward. "Uh, thanks, Eddie, but I'm seeing someone at the moment, but I really appreciate you asking."

"A guy's gotta ask or kick himself for not trying. Have a nice day." He pulled out and drove away.

"Hey, Katie!" Big John bellowed from the front door. "I've got some great news for you."

"Hit me with the good news, John!"

"We are almost done with the outside, just need to paint up the front tomorrow. The roof is repaired, but we do have to do some repair work around the chimney tomorrow or maybe the next day. Looks like there's a leak we'll fix up. Then the roofers will do the roof next week, ahead of schedule—"

"Wow, that is great, John!" Katie said. She was impressed that it was at least a week ahead of schedule. "Why so many guys here today?"

"Well, let me finish first. We'd like to get guys in tomorrow to work on the upstairs. That ceilin' is a mess. That's gonna take some plaster work, but I got the best guy for that. He's not fast. In fact, he's kinda slow, but nobody can touch him. It's like I went back in time to the 1800s to get him."

"Fabulous."

"Okay. Another job my boys are working on got stalled on a permit. I don't like my boys not workin', on account they've got families to feed, so I figured I'd get their asses here. Didn't think you'd mind."

John rubbed his nose on his sleeve. "Plants in front of the house are toast. As we spoke about, I'm gonna get you some nice new ones. Sorry 'bout that, they aren't cheap, but I got a good line on some nice plants."

"How was your lunch meeting yesterday?" Katie asked. She didn't really care, but Big John was a loveable and caring man, so she thought the small talk would help.

"Oh. Great. Those boys can eat me out of a lot of pizza. But they can share with me concerns they have and we all remain family. Some of these guys have been with me for thirty years. They are loyal," he said. Then he laughed.

"What?"

"Well, a couple of the boys are nervous about coming inside tomorrow on account of the ghosts." He let out a bellowing laugh.

"Ghosts."

"Well, old houses, some people think, have 'em. I said I'd tell you about Psychic Diana and get her to scare them away." He laughed more. He was having a great laugh over this.

Katie wasn't laughing. It was annoying her. "I'm sorry, miss. I'm just having fun..."

"Did Mel set you up for this? Are there hidden cameras here?"

"No, cameras won't be set up until later—"

"No, I mean are you playing a joke on me?"

John looked uncomfortable. Uncomfortable like he'd just pissed off his client and would lose business over it. Like he'd talked about politics or religion when he shouldn't have.

"No ma'am. Sorry if I have offended you. I'm—"

Katie took a breath and realized she was overreacting. *This is stupid*, she thought. "No, John, it's okay. I'm just getting tired of being teased about ghosts. That's all. Really, I'm not mad at you."

John let out a big sigh. "Okay, miss. I'm sorry. Anyways, I'm gonna get the guys movin' along. I'll be in later to fix up the security system."

***

Katie felt safe in the house with everyone around, but the air seemed... thin. A feeling of it being hard to breathe at times. Not everywhere, just certain places. Like in front of the fireplace.

Nonsense, girl. I'm just imagining this now that I know about the murders. There's no such thing as ghosts. Besides, this took place decades ago. Smarten up... she thought, giving herself a pep-talk.

I need to pee. Katie went to the washroom on the main floor, but unfortunately one of the workers had used it before her.

"Holy hell, what do you guys eat?" she asked out loud. She headed upstairs, and on the way up she ran her hand up the old bannister and wondered how many people had held this same one over the years. *They're sure going to look magnificent when they get a cleaning and new coat of stain.*

The bathroom door clunked behind her and she quickly sat down. A slight draft was coming in through the old windowsill. Another thing that would need to be fixed. The air was fresh and she could smell the ever-so-faint scent of lavender.

Frozen in place, Katie looked at the bottom of the door as an unmistakable shadow passed by.

"I'm in the bathroom. Who's there, please?" she said, loudly.

The scent became stronger. She took a deep breath and held it and felt her heart pounding on the left side of her neck.

"Hello?"

Katie stared at the bottom of the door. Whomever had gone by had gone in the direction of her bedroom. No mistaking that. If this was a joke, she was getting angry about it. Could it be a worker who didn't speak English? Not likely, she reasoned, as they'd at least say something.

Katie took a deep breath, jumped up while simultaneously yanking up her jeans, and dashed for the door. Someone was about to get an earful of hell from a very upset woman.

Her hand slammed the door handle and with a flick of her wrist she swung the door inward and dashed out into the hallway. The door smashed into the edge of the old lion claw tub and she darted down the hall, glancing quickly into Mel's room. There was nobody in there. She continued her motion into her bedroom.

"I said, who's there?"

Other than the sound of the workers outside, the house was silent.

Skeptical of even her own thoughts, she walked towards the closet and swung the door open. Nothing. She peeked underneath her bed. Still nothing.

I'm losing my mind. I am. Losing. My mind.

She walked quickly back to Mel's room and did a double check. There was nobody in the room. She went and stood in the dark hallway looking both ways.

The stairs, although very sturdy, gave a very distinct creak as you came up them. There was no way anybody could've come up or gone back down without her hearing.

"That settles it. I'm nuts," she said. She wasn't sure whether she was half joking or half serious. She did know this: the house was getting to her.

Katie headed back downstairs to the kitchen. She sat down in her chair and looked out the window. It was an old wooden chair, no padding. But it was the most comfortable chair she'd ever sat in in a kitchen. She leaned back and rested her arm on the kitchen table.

There were many good hotels and motels in town. It wouldn't be the first time that she'd stayed in a beautiful hotel and used it as a write-off. It would be tax deductible, so maybe that's what she needed to do. As she was mulling it over, Katie glanced down at the kitchen table where she had dropped the business card. It was lying face down. She picked it up and turned it over and laughed.

I cannot believe I'm thinking about calling in a psychic, she thought to herself. If she ever needed proof that she was nuts, the phone call would be that proof.

CHAPTER EIGHT

The only room left available to book at the Sedona spa and hotel was a suite. Way too large for what she needed, but it was beautiful. The suite was large and spacious, with a living room and a separate bedroom. The living room overlooked the lake and was just five minutes from Mel's place.

Mel would certainly be upset that she was booked into a hotel. Katie was expecting that. But she just needed some time to be alone, away from the house, to think about things.

She wanted this house gone. That she loved it was no question. But it was getting to her. The house seemed almost alive and resistant to change.

If the house could talk, it would probably tell her to get out. She decided there and then—even before ordering room service—she would follow the min/max solution: do the minimum amount of work and get the maximum amount of benefit from it.

Katie decided to treat herself. She ordered a filet mignon and garlic mashed potatoes with a side of veggies. And a bottle of wine.

Katie pulled out the chair from the desk and brought it over to the window. It was a high-end office style chair of the type that she preferred. She sat down and watched the sun setting over the lake.

She tilted the chair back slightly and put her feet up on the ledge of the windowsill. She felt a little guilty doing so, but for the amount of money that she was paying for the room and the ungodly cost of the meal, she deserved a little luxury.

Katie started talking to herself out loud as she was prone to do when she was by herself and knew nobody could hear.

"Okay. I'm agnostic. I'm not an atheist, but I can't wrap my head around there being a God. Therefore no heaven. Therefore no dead people to haunt me..."

Katie held her left hand up palm up as she spoke, like some sort of scale of justice. It would probably look weird to somebody watching, but it worked for her.

"It's tragic, but those people died a long, long time ago. And dead people are dead," she said. She laughed out loud at the profundity of that statement. "Wow."

She lowered her left hand and raised her right hand palm up. Time to stack some stuff on the other side of the scale.

"Okay, this is silly, but if there are ghosts, why are they so upset? I'm fixing up the place, I'm restoring its natural beauty, the memories of these people will live on. Wouldn't that be what they want?"

She dropped her arms and gazed out, watching the sunset on the horizon. She waited till it was almost jet black before she closed the curtains. Katie had started to get a little agitated at how long it was taking for the room service when suddenly the door knock occurred.

"Good evening!" the young lady said. She rolled in a portable table, popped up the sides and removed the lid to show an absolutely gorgeously laid meal. The woman deftly popped the cork on the wine bottle and poured a sample. Katie waved off a taste test and signed the bill, adding a generous tip. "Thank you very much. Please give us a call when you're done and we'll come and collect the dishes. Have a good night."

The steak was incredibly tender. It sliced like butter and melted in her mouth. She deserved it, she had earned it. Her wine was a local Merlot that paired perfectly with the steak. The garlic mashed potatoes were perfectly delicious.

Katie hadn't realized how hungry she really was. She enjoyed every bite and was amazed at how quickly she ate. She rolled the portable table out into the hallway, closed and locked the door and stripped down for the night. She poured herself another glass of wine and hopped on her king-size bed.

She picked up the business card again. She looked at it. *Psychic Diana? Let's give this chick a call,* she thought to herself.

Maybe it was too late. It was 7:30 PM, after all. The phone rang three times and Katie considered hanging up, but then someone did pick up the phone.

"Psychic Diana. How can I help you?"

"Hey. I uhhhh. I've never done anything like this before. I'm calling to find out about how you do housecleaning?"

The lady on the end of the line laughed. Hard. "Well, you won't catch me doing any housecleaning. My own place is a hard enough mess," Diana said.

Both ladies laughed out loud for a minute. "Okay, okay. Sorry, that's not what I meant—"

"That's okay. You're talking about house cleansing?"

"Absolutely. You are highly recommended from a friend of mine by the name of Mel Wragg. But I have to tell you, I'm highly skeptical of the stuff. No offense."

"No offense taken at all. When you do this kind of work you have to expect people to not understand it. But it's along the same lines as babies getting baptized, blessing burials, or thanksgiving prayers. It's much the same. Just think of it as a ritual. I'm the first to tell people that if you believe, great. If you don't believe, what does it hurt to have your house blessed?"

"Cool. Are you a witch or something?"

The woman laughed again. "No, I'm not which, not that there's anything wrong with them. Only a spiritual advisor—actually I'm a reverend, to be honest—and I can legally marry people, for example. And I am a psychic"

"So how does a blessing work?"

"It's pretty straightforward. I come to your house and I burn sage. Using a feather I wave the smoke into all areas of the house and I ask that God bless the house. God's divine energy will fill the house, and if there's any negative energies they will be gone."

"Negative energies? Like ghosts or bogeyman?"

Katie didn't realize it, but her negative approach was grating on Diana. It's one thing to question somebody, but it's another to be argumentative. Diana decided to take a different tack.

"I'm assuming that this is a new house for you. But my intuition tells me that you don't intend to stay long. I feel like the house that you're looking at is quite large. Way more than you need or even feel comfortable in. Yes, that's it. I feel you're looking at an old house, very old..."

Katie bit her lip. She was familiar with the old magic trick of cold reading. Diana had just described pretty much any house in the area. Maybe this was just one big con job after all. That said, Katie hadn't said what her name was, and her phone was blocked so no name would be showing up on Diana's caller ID. And even if she was quick enough to use a computer to look up the phone number, it would show that it was from out of state. She decided to listen to what the lady had to say.

"I'm sensing a lot of heaviness at this house. Much tragedy has fallen on this home. There is a lot of negative energy there..."

Katie was shaking her head. Such bull crap.

"You bought the Blackstone house!" Diana said. The exclamation in her voice startled Katie.

"Did Mel put you up to this? She highly recommended you, so she probably told you that I was buying the house and you probably deduced that it was me."

"Look. I'm going to be blunt with you. I have a stellar reputation and no need to bullshit anybody. You obviously are not a believer, and that's fine. Let's agree not to waste each other's time. Have a good evening."

Before Katie could utter a word Diana hung up the phone.

"Bullshit."

Katie was livid now. She immediately dialed Mel.

"Hey, chickipoo, how—"

"What's going on, Mel? Why are you messing with me with this ghost stuff?"

"What do you mean?"

"The business card, the taxi driver, all of this ghost crap. I can't believe I'm telling you this, but I called her up and she knew who I was, even knew that I bought the Blackstone house. What else did you tell her?"

"Calm the hell down. I told her nothing. I figured it would help you out, put your mind at ease. I have business cards from all kinds of suppliers, from draperies, interior decorators, construction workers, electricians, you name it. You know that. I also have the business card of the psychic that does house cleansings. Weird. I know. But you're experiencing some weird shit there—"

"Are you saying that you never told her about me?"

"The only people in the know who bought that house are the lawyers, Christopher Watkin, you and me. Well, of course Big John knows now, but that's it. You need to chill. Everyone has nightmares. Everyone sees shadows. You're in a spooky house, no two ways about it—"

"Spooky is right. It really is haunting me, Mel."

"Just because you have a weird dream doesn't mean there's ghosts."

"You had a dream when you were at my place. Tell me about that..."

"I can barely remember it now."

"Were you in bare feet? Did you walk outside? Did you walk over to the willow tree?"

"That's pretty much how I remember it," said Mel.

"Well, problem is, you didn't tell me your dream. And that's the exact dream that I've been having over and over again at the house. Each time I have that dream it gets worse and worse—"

"Oh my God. Are you serious? Are you pulling my leg now?"

"I'm dead serious. The dream becomes more vivid, clearer details each time, it feels more real each time. And the thing that haunts me the most is the screams. I'm outside and I can't do anything to save the people from dying."

"You are freaking me out," Mel said.

"I'm freaking out. How can we both have the exact same nightmare? Right down to the little tiny details?"

"I have no idea," Mel said. "I swear to you, Katie, I didn't tell Psychic Diana anything. Sure, what she does might be strange, but I think she's every bit as legit as the Pope. I know you're not a believer in religion, but having her in might make you feel better. Besides, it would be a tax write-off for you..."

Katie laughed. "I guess this is tax write-off day for me."

***

The following morning Katie felt better. Although Mel was worried about her—she'd never known her to be this agitated and snappy—Katie felt much more alive. She didn't believe in ghosts or goblins, but she did know this: she felt better being away from the house. It was a downer.

Katie jumped in the shower and took her time. It was hot, it was fresh and the soaps and shampoos in the marble stall were orange-citrus scented. She loved it.

There was high-end coffee in her room and she made herself two cups. Wearing a comfortable, cozy robe, she sat down to observe the lake and make a call.

"Diana. Hi, this is Katie. I spoke with you last night and I wanted to apologize to you. I've had a crazy couple of days, and while that's not an excuse, I realize I was rude to you. I wouldn't call the Pope and mock his beliefs and I shouldn't mock yours—"

"Stop apologizing. I had a client from hell, so to speak, and I was a bit edgy yesterday too. How can I be of help?"

"Well, I do happen to own the Blackstone house and I would love for you to come and do a cleansing. When can you come by?"

"I can come by today if you like, or tomorrow."

"Tomorrow would be better. I've got workers working on the place. Do you need quiet or nighttime or what—"

"Nothing special. But I would like to bring a friend if that's okay. There have been stories over the years, and if there is any negative energy, she's great at getting that stuff out. No extra charge. How does 3:00 PM sound?"

"I'll see you then! And thank you," Katie hung up the phone and, curiously, felt a lot better. *Like Mel said, even if it's psychological, feeling better is the name of the game.* Surely, things would go better now.

CHAPTER NINE

Katie drove up the long road to the house. As she rounded the bend she nearly cried tears of joy. The outside was finished and completely restored. She parked and climbed out.

Absentmindedly, she walked around the car and walked in the direction of the willow tree. The house looked postcard perfect.

Sure, it needed more work. She realized that this was just the cosmetics, but cosmetics sold when you flipped houses. Curb appeal was everything, and this house had it. It had the magic for a flip: it was beautiful.

Wow, Big John even got the new bushes installed. Wow.

As she stood in the yard looking at the house, Big John pulled up in his massive diesel truck.

"Hey, Big John!"

"Hey, missy, how do you like the job that the boys did?"

"Oh my God, John, the house is absolutely beautiful. It looks brand-new, like we stepped back in time," Katie said. She was beaming with joy.

John rubbed his nose on his arm. "Thank you. The boys worked really hard, and I'm glad that we kept your vision, because it turned out much nicer than I thought it would. The woodwork took a lot of prep but we managed to save most of it, and the whitewash is just beautiful. Come here," he said, gesturing for her to follow him.

For a brief moment, the roles reversed and it seemed as though Big John was the proud owner showing off his home. Katie was enjoying it.

He continued, enthusiastically. "Look at the gorgeous trim work. The craftsmen back in those days paid a lot of attention to detail, but look over the doorway..."

Katie looked up and was stunned at what she saw. Was this new? Had it always been there and she'd missed it? It was just beautiful. "Wow, Big John..."

They both stood looking at the black oval plaque above the door with the raised old style script. It was painted in gold—the letter 'B'.

"Blackstone Manor, Katie."

The front door looked unfinished, but before Katie could comment on it John spoke. "And we'll have the door done by the end of the day. It needs to stay propped open to dry, and we ran out of time yesterday."

Big John was beaming. He felt a sense of pride in both his work and knowing that his client was thrilled. He rubbed his nose with the back of his arm and stood with his hands on his hips looking up at the great old home.

Suddenly he remembered, "Oh, I've got something for you. Let's head inside."

Katie opened the door with her key, but Big John swung it open wide, which she thought was a bit strange and borderline rude. He had always been a gentleman up to this point.

But she didn't see what he'd seen only moments before.

As they'd walked up to the gorgeous front porch, John had seen what seemed to be a reflection—or maybe the shadow—of a person by the door side window. Maybe a friend of Katie's? Or an early worker?

Big John stepped in in front of Katie and immediately looked behind the door and scanned the library. The house was empty. He said nothing, instead keeping on with the conversation underway.

"We set up the security cameras for the outside and inside too. One of my boys knows computers and rigged everything up yesterday. Made it look easy. He left this paper so that you can watch it from your computer on the phone network."

Katie let out a silent giggle. Phone network? He really had no clue about computers. She glanced at the paper and it gave a website address and password so she could access the system, which she planned to do later.

As they spoke, two pickup trucks pulled up. The door was wide open, letting a breeze of much needed fresh air into the house.

"What are the plans for today, Big John?"

"Well, we're going to make that door look pretty, as I mentioned. It'll be bright red and the brass will make it stand out. Beautiful against the white and black shutters.

"The boys will be very busy fixing the upstairs first, work our way downstairs. We have a couple of weeks left of work, but it's going faster than expected.

"There's a leak on the roof—"

"How bad?"

"Not bad now, but it will get flagged if inspected and worse if it's not dealt with. Jason and I are going to head up there and take a gander at it. We'll have that fixed up tonight."

John seemed distracted as he was speaking. He kept looking in the kitchen, which he could partly see from his vantage point near the fireplace. He said nothing, but Katie noticed.

John continued, "This place is going to be back to its former glory in no time. Whoever gets this place is going to love it—"

John and Katie looked at each other as they heard what sounded at first like chimes... the chimes got louder, but it wasn't chimes, it was the sound of glasses and dishes rattling in the kitchen.

"Earthquake," John said calmly, as the shaking got stronger.

Katie put her hand on the mantle of the fireplace and her eyes were as big as saucers. *How the hell can you be so calm,* she thought.

"You okay, missy?" said John.

"This house doesn't like change," Katie said matter-of-factly.

John gave her a quizzical look. How do you answer that?

Katie slowly looked around the library. Everything looked fine. Since everything was off of the shelves, there was nothing to fall or break. She had a bad feeling.

John headed outside. Katie raised up her right hand and rubbed her left shoulder and neck. She was tense and tight. This had been building all morning and the house shaking didn't help.

Walking into the kitchen, she got the coffee maker going and leaned against the kitchen counter. The smell of fresh coffee filled the air. Looking over at the kitchen table she noticed that her chair was pulled out. Weird, as she always put chairs back... she was practically OCD about that. *Probably one of the guys left it out*, she tried to convince herself.

With the coffee finally brewed she opened the overhead cupboard containing the cups. A ceramic cup fell and first hit the counter, snapping off its handle, before falling to the floor and smashing into five big pieces.

For a brief second, Katie was startled. Anyone would be. After all, the whole house had just shaken and the cup had probably shifted.

But Katie simply looked down and stared at the broken pieces. She stared at them with a bizarre calm fear. That same sense her Uncle Ray must have had when he was dying of cancer: afraid, but calmly facing his inevitable death.

This is a bad place. A very bad place.

Katie got another cup and filled it with coffee. She took a sip and wondered where the dustpan and broom were. It was remarkably quiet. As she looked out the window at the forest she wondered if John Blackstone was still out there, watching from the bushes. She shuddered at the thought. *I'll get you before you get me...*

The silence was suddenly broken by a knock at the door. Several guys were standing on the porch. Different men. "Can we come in, ma'am? We're starting work upstairs."

"Guys, come and go as you please, no need to knock, okay?"

Katie cleaned up the broken cup and sat down at the kitchen table with the laptop. She logged in and, after a few initial errors, finally got the system working and was amazed to see the security cameras in action.

Outside the cameras showed the full back part of the house, both sides and two views of the front. Katie was impressed.

Inside the camera was mounted in the back of the library. It was a 'fish eye' camera and showed the front door, the entire library including the staircase, and the doorway to the kitchen. If someone broke into the kitchen or front, they'd never be able to bypass the camera.

Katie saw a camera named 'remote' and clicked on it. A screen popped up on her laptop showing... the attic. Cool. It looked to be put in a corner. It didn't show the door, but was angled in such a way that you could see most of the room, including the mouse traps still on the floor.

Katie took another sip of coffee and leaned back in her chair. She did feel a bit more secure, but the feeling of something ominous was still upon her.

It was beginning to get noisy. The men upstairs were talking loudly and one of them obviously had a portable stereo as it was belting out AC/DC music. Two other guys were in the library prepping the bookcases for staining.

Mid-sip of her almost finished coffee a loud noise was heard outside, followed by two successive thuds... then the unmistakable sound of a ladder crashing to the ground.

The two men in the library raced outside without saying a word. Two more men came barreling down the stairs with one saying to the other, "Sounded like a lightning bolt!"

Katie jumped to her feet and ran out the front door to pandemonium.

"Call 911. Quick!" yelled one of the workers; Katie didn't know his name.

"What happened?" she yelled back at him.

"Two men fell from the roof!" he shouted back, although he was only two feet from Katie. He was panicked.

Oh my God. Big John—

"My phone is dead, someone call 911 NOW!"

Katie was now standing at the right side of the house. She saw the body of Big John lying face up on the grass, the ladder not far from him. His left leg was twisted completely the wrong way. His face was bleeding.

Katie realized her phone was in her jeans, so she reached into her back pocket and dialed 911.

"Jason isn't breathing!" screamed one of the guys, the one who was panicking. Another guy ran over, nudged him out of the way and began performing CPR. Katie walked over while giving details to the 911 operator.

"Please hurry, one has stopped breathing!" Katie hung up and yelled at the guys trying to wake up Big John, "Don't shake him or move him, his back might be broken..."

Katie suddenly started to cry. She'd grown fond of Big John; his habit of calling her 'missy' and even his disgusting nose rubbing had endeared him to her. "Please don't let him die," she prayed out loud.

Katie walked over to the first guy she saw outside. "What happened?"

The guy, an older man in maybe his 50s, was clearly in shock. He was holding a portable camera with the lens still extended. "I... I... it happened so fast. Big John asked me to take some pictures of the front of the house so we can use them to promote. I was facing the front and I heard a loud 'CRACK' sound. Like a bolt of lightning. I saw Jason jump... no... he was thrown from the chimney. I ran around and I saw that John was there too. He must have been shocked too."

Jason was lying quite a distance from Big John. Katie couldn't figure out how John had ended up on the ground, but there he was and he wasn't looking good at all. They were still performing CPR on Jason.

"Can you show me the pictures?" Katie said. The guy looked at her like she had just asked the most inappropriate question in the world. "To see if you caught the shock on camera, not for the house pics!"

The man pressed a few buttons to pull up the last shots and handed the camera to her. Sure enough, there was Jason crouched down by the chimney. And holy hell, there he was, airborne, looking like a limp rag!

Unfortunately, the next two shots were of the ground and the bushes. Clearly the man had kept his finger on the shutter button but was dropping the camera at that point.

Two ambulances and a police car pulled up. First to move was Jason. They evacuated him quickly and were still giving him CPR when they closed the doors and pulled away.

Katie walked beside John when they wheeled him to the ambulance. She grabbed his hand, but he was out cold. The attendant said they would do all they could for him.

Please don't let them die, God. Please... Katie burst into tears. She had never felt so helpless in all her life.

CHAPTER TEN

"Thank you for being so patient and letting us use your kitchen for the interviews," Officer Rinaldo said. "I don't know if you are aware, but the young man passed away—"

"Oh my God... how's Big John?"

"He's in rough shape but fully expected to survive. Don't know all the details, but he's got a bad concussion, broken ribs and a badly broken leg—"

"Is he awake?"

"I don't know at this point, but there was no sense of there being an emergency. It's a miracle he's alive," the officer said, in a stereotypical tone of trained calm.

"What happened?"

"That's what I'm here to investigate. You are the new homeowner, correct?"

"Yes, but I was in here. The guy who took the photos said it looked like he was electrocuted and thrown—"

"Yes, I spoke to him. So, where were you?"

"I was inside. In fact, in here."

"Perfect. That's all we have for now."

"Jeez. Are we suspects or something?" Katie said. She didn't like the questioning.

"Relax. Around here we have to dot our 'i's' and cross our 't's.' We need an accounting of everyone. Procedure. It was just a terrible accident."

Katie shifted in her chair. "Well, on or off the record, what the hell happened, do you think... or know?"

"At this point, my guess would be the leak made contact with some electricity. There was an old TV antenna up there that wasn't properly removed. The deceased definitely had an electrical burn on his leg and a broken neck. That is some fall, let me say—"

"And Big John? He was climbing a ladder—"

"The young guy hit the top of the roof and slid, hitting the top of John's ladder, and knocked it off the roof. John went with it."

Officer Rinaldo gave Katie his card and left. The guys were all standing outside around one of the pickup trucks. Katie went out to see how they were doing. One of them, Pedro, spoke.

"Ma'am. This is a terrible shock to us. We have known both hombres for a long time. We are so sorry this happened to you here today. But we have spoken and we would like to ask if it would be okay to continue working for you today."

Katie was shocked. It showed on her face clearly.

"Mister John spoke highly of you. We are sad, yes. But we can all go home and be sad or we can work and be sad. Jason loved to work and I believe Big John would want us to not worry and work for you today. Please."

Katie agreed. It felt weird, but they were all in consensus. As she walked back to the house, her cell phone rang.

"Hey, it's Psychic Diana," she cheerfully said. "Just confirming our appointment today."

Katie answered awkwardly. "Uh. Sorry, a worker was killed on site here today, and Big John was badly injured. I should have called you but I completely forgot—"

"Nonsense. Don't apologize. That's horrible. Are you okay?"

"Well, I'm in shock, but I'm getting freaked out. Like, very freaked out."

"Can I suggest something? Let me come by tomorrow morning. A house cleansing doesn't take that long and it'll change the energy. There's a lot of death around there. Let me see if there are any spirits hanging around and let me send them to the light. Seriously."

"Okay. Perfect. Just call first. Talk tomorrow. Bye," Katie said. For the first time ever in her short life, that conversation could actually feel normal. Weird, but normal. She would have laughed that lady out of town two weeks ago. *Now I'm having her get rid of dead people for me. Right. That's normal.*

No sooner did she hang up than the phone rang again. It was Mel. "Heyyyyy, chick—"

"Big John is in the hospital and one of his workers is dead—electrocuted at my house—I'm freaking out here—"

"Whoa. Slow down. What?"

Katie caught her up quickly with all the details. "I'm going to the hospital to see him now—"

"Wait. I'm driving close to your place now, just listed a house. Let me pick you up and we'll go together."

"Sounds great. I'll see you soon."

Mel arrived in short order. As they drove, they each shared their shock. Mel was just as stunned as Katie. She asked her to give her every detail and Katie did so. Katie clearly needed to vent and Mel let her get it out. It made the 25-minute drive go by faster.

Both ladies were surprised to find out that Big John was awake but sedated for pain and that they were allowed in to visit.

Big John looked terrible. His leg was raised up in a full length cast. He had a cast on his right hand wrapping his little finger and ring finger. A large bandage was stuck to the right side of his face and there was a wrap around his head. He also had a black eye and partially swollen lip.

The ladies were in shock at the sorry sight of him, and doubly shocked when he popped open his eyes and gave a cheerful, "Ladies! Good to see ya both. How is your day going?"

He was trying to be funny, and the ladies both gave a brave smile, but that was quickly broken when Mel started crying.

"Oh, don't cry, Mel. I'm going to be okay. Really. This is nuthin'."

"I'm so sorry this happened to you, Big John," Mel said.

"Me too, John," Katie said.

"Listen, there's somethin' I need to tell you both. I saw a shadow in your living room and kitchen when I was there. It was on the roof and threw Jason at me..."

Both ladies were stunned. They both looked at each other.

"Look. I'm on strong stuff right now, but I'm not imagining it. I don't know what it was, but it didn't like Jason being there."

Both ladies kept quiet. Neither mentioned Jason had died, and they were unsure if he knew or not.

A nurse came in and politely asked them both to leave as his blood pressure was quite high.

"We love you, Big John," Mel said.

"I love you too. Oh, please tell the guys to stick to the schedule. No time off on account of me," he said. He let out a pained laugh while holding his broken ribs.

Mel and Katie exited the room and Mel suggested a cup of coffee in the cafeteria, which apparently was quite good. "That boy is tough as they come. Wasn't sure if he knew of Jason or not—"

"I was thinking exactly the same, Mel. Listen. Be honest with me, is he one of those woo-woo believing people?"

"You mean, does he believe in ghosts? That I don't know, but I can tell you this: he's a straight shooter. If he says he saw something, he saw something—BUT—and this is a big but... he had a concussion. He might be mis-remembering things.

"Well. I can tell you this. I spoke to him when he first arrived. He was chirpy and cheerful. Happy as Larry. We were admiring the great job he did on the house—"

"The house is incredible," Mel said, interrupting. "Sorry. Go on."

"Thanks. It is beautiful. He changed when we got in the house. He was looking around, almost as though looking for someone hiding. I didn't see anything. Hard to describe."

"Like, skitterish?"

"No. More like suspicious... that's not the word... just a vibe of having seen something out of the corner of your eye and not knowing if it was real or imagined."

"Okay. That's unusual. What did he say it was?"

"He said nothing."

"Well, that's weird," said Mel. They ordered their coffees to go and headed back to Mel's car.

They drove in silence for nearly ten minutes before Mel spoke up again. "Did you call Psychic Diana?"

"Yes. She was to come today, but with the mess, she's coming tomorrow. Says there's a bunch of dead people that might be hanging around."

Mel was amazed at how matter-of-fact her statement was. "Well, it's not going to hurt having it done. Even if it's just superstitious. Like baptizing a kid. Doesn't matter if you believe or not, it can't hurt any."

"I guess so," Katie said. Her mind was far off.

"Why don't you stay at my place for a few days?"

"I can't tonight, I'm booked into the Sedona Spa—"

"Why are you booked in there? You could have stayed at my place," Mel said, a bit indignantly.

"Hey, a lot was going on and I didn't want to be an imposition."

"Let's clear something up. You are not an imposition. Okay? You come to my place. Besides, I've got free wine. That place charges more for a bottle than a motel does for a night!"

That broke the ice. Both ladies laughed hard.

***

Katie locked up the house, set the new alarm and headed to the Sedona Spa to pick up her stuff. It was too late to cancel, but she felt it would be better hanging out at Mel's for the next several days.

Turned out to be a good decision. While it wasn't fun, it wasn't gloomy either. Mel made up a pizza from scratch and cooked it in her BBQ on the back deck. Red wine flowed and they rehashed the day's events. It was good to get the shock out of Katie's system.

Mel phoned the hospital at 8:30 PM and spoke to a nurse she knew there.

"Good news, chickie, Big John is expected to make a full recovery. No brain damage, just a concussion. Everything else is going to heal, but he is in a lot of pain right now and his blood pressure is up there. He's medicated for that. He's going to be okay, we just need to be patient," Mel reported.

"Thank goodness. That is a relief. Wow. A huge relief. I'll drink to that."

"Cheers," Mel said.

The ladies both agreed to change topics for a while. Mel got her caught up to date on the latest listing from the morning and some of the gossip from her office.

"Did you feel the earthquake this morning?" Katie asked.

"What? What earthquake?"

"Well, maybe it was just a tremor, but it made the house shake," Katie said.

Mel pulled out her phone and did a quick search. "No earthquakes or tremors recorded anywhere near our area today," she said.

Katie looked Mel straight in the eyes. "There was at Blackstone Manor."

After a long pause, Mel said, "We need to get you out of there."

CHAPTER ELEVEN

"Thank you for being so patient and letting us use your kitchen for the interviews," Officer Rinaldo said. "I don't know if you are aware, but the young man passed away—"

"Oh my God... how's Big John?"

"He's in rough shape but fully expected to survive. Don't know all the details, but he's got a bad concussion, broken ribs and a badly broken leg—"

"Is he awake?"

"I don't know at this point, but there was no sense of there being an emergency. It's a miracle he's alive," the officer said, in a stereotypical tone of trained calm.

"What happened?"

"That's what I'm here to investigate. You are the new homeowner, correct?"

"Yes, but I was in here. The guy who took the photos said it looked like he was electrocuted and thrown—"

"Yes, I spoke to him. So, where were you?"

"I was inside. In fact, in here."

"Perfect. That's all we have for now."

"Jeez. Are we suspects or something?" Katie said. She didn't like the questioning.

"Relax. Around here we have to dot our 'i's' and cross our 't's.' We need an accounting of everyone. Procedure. It was just a terrible accident."

Katie shifted in her chair. "Well, on or off the record, what the hell happened, do you think... or know?"

"At this point, my guess would be the leak made contact with some electricity. There was an old TV antenna up there that wasn't properly removed. The deceased definitely had an electrical burn on his leg and a broken neck. That is some fall, let me say—"

"And Big John? He was climbing a ladder—"

"The young guy hit the top of the roof and slid, hitting the top of John's ladder, and knocked it off the roof. John went with it."

Officer Rinaldo gave Katie his card and left. The guys were all standing outside around one of the pickup trucks. Katie went out to see how they were doing. One of them, Pedro, spoke.

"Ma'am. This is a terrible shock to us. We have known both hombres for a long time. We are so sorry this happened to you here today. But we have spoken and we would like to ask if it would be okay to continue working for you today."

Katie was shocked. It showed on her face clearly.

"Mister John spoke highly of you. We are sad, yes. But we can all go home and be sad or we can work and be sad. Jason loved to work and I believe Big John would want us to not worry and work for you today. Please."

Katie agreed. It felt weird, but they were all in consensus. As she walked back to the house, her cell phone rang.

"Hey, it's Psychic Diana," she cheerfully said. "Just confirming our appointment today."

Katie answered awkwardly. "Uh. Sorry, a worker was killed on site here today, and Big John was badly injured. I should have called you but I completely forgot—"

"Nonsense. Don't apologize. That's horrible. Are you okay?"

"Well, I'm in shock, but I'm getting freaked out. Like, very freaked out."

"Can I suggest something? Let me come by tomorrow morning. A house cleansing doesn't take that long and it'll change the energy. There's a lot of death around there. Let me see if there are any spirits hanging around and let me send them to the light. Seriously."

"Okay. Perfect. Just call first. Talk tomorrow. Bye," Katie said. For the first time ever in her short life, that conversation could actually feel normal. Weird, but normal. She would have laughed that lady out of town two weeks ago. *Now I'm having her get rid of dead people for me. Right. That's normal.*

No sooner did she hang up than the phone rang again. It was Mel. "Heyyyyy, chick—"

"Big John is in the hospital and one of his workers is dead—electrocuted at my house—I'm freaking out here—"

"Whoa. Slow down. What?"

Katie caught her up quickly with all the details. "I'm going to the hospital to see him now—"

"Wait. I'm driving close to your place now, just listed a house. Let me pick you up and we'll go together."

"Sounds great. I'll see you soon."

Mel arrived in short order. As they drove, they each shared their shock. Mel was just as stunned as Katie. She asked her to give her every detail and Katie did so. Katie clearly needed to vent and Mel let her get it out. It made the 25-minute drive go by faster.

Both ladies were surprised to find out that Big John was awake but sedated for pain and that they were allowed in to visit.

Big John looked terrible. His leg was raised up in a full length cast. He had a cast on his right hand wrapping his little finger and ring finger. A large bandage was stuck to the right side of his face and there was a wrap around his head. He also had a black eye and partially swollen lip.

The ladies were in shock at the sorry sight of him, and doubly shocked when he popped open his eyes and gave a cheerful, "Ladies! Good to see ya both. How is your day going?"

He was trying to be funny, and the ladies both gave a brave smile, but that was quickly broken when Mel started crying.

"Oh, don't cry, Mel. I'm going to be okay. Really. This is nuthin'."

"I'm so sorry this happened to you, Big John," Mel said.

"Me too, John," Katie said.

"Listen, there's somethin' I need to tell you both. I saw a shadow in your living room and kitchen when I was there. It was on the roof and threw Jason at me..."

Both ladies were stunned. They both looked at each other.

"Look. I'm on strong stuff right now, but I'm not imagining it. I don't know what it was, but it didn't like Jason being there."

Both ladies kept quiet. Neither mentioned Jason had died, and they were unsure if he knew or not.

A nurse came in and politely asked them both to leave as his blood pressure was quite high.

"We love you, Big John," Mel said.

"I love you too. Oh, please tell the guys to stick to the schedule. No time off on account of me," he said. He let out a pained laugh while holding his broken ribs.

Mel and Katie exited the room and Mel suggested a cup of coffee in the cafeteria, which apparently was quite good. "That boy is tough as they come. Wasn't sure if he knew of Jason or not—"

"I was thinking exactly the same, Mel. Listen. Be honest with me, is he one of those woo-woo believing people?"

"You mean, does he believe in ghosts? That I don't know, but I can tell you this: he's a straight shooter. If he says he saw something, he saw something—BUT—and this is a big but... he had a concussion. He might be mis-remembering things.

"Well. I can tell you this. I spoke to him when he first arrived. He was chirpy and cheerful. Happy as Larry. We were admiring the great job he did on the house—"

"The house is incredible," Mel said, interrupting. "Sorry. Go on."

"Thanks. It is beautiful. He changed when we got in the house. He was looking around, almost as though looking for someone hiding. I didn't see anything. Hard to describe."

"Like, skitterish?"

"No. More like suspicious... that's not the word... just a vibe of having seen something out of the corner of your eye and not knowing if it was real or imagined."

"Okay. That's unusual. What did he say it was?"

"He said nothing."

"Well, that's weird," said Mel. They ordered their coffees to go and headed back to Mel's car.

They drove in silence for nearly ten minutes before Mel spoke up again. "Did you call Psychic Diana?"

"Yes. She was to come today, but with the mess, she's coming tomorrow. Says there's a bunch of dead people that might be hanging around."

Mel was amazed at how matter-of-fact her statement was. "Well, it's not going to hurt having it done. Even if it's just superstitious. Like baptizing a kid. Doesn't matter if you believe or not, it can't hurt any."

"I guess so," Katie said. Her mind was far off.

"Why don't you stay at my place for a few days?"

"I can't tonight, I'm booked into the Sedona Spa—"

"Why are you booked in there? You could have stayed at my place," Mel said, a bit indignantly.

"Hey, a lot was going on and I didn't want to be an imposition."

"Let's clear something up. You are not an imposition. Okay? You come to my place. Besides, I've got free wine. That place charges more for a bottle than a motel does for a night!"

That broke the ice. Both ladies laughed hard.

***

Katie locked up the house, set the new alarm and headed to the Sedona Spa to pick up her stuff. It was too late to cancel, but she felt it would be better hanging out at Mel's for the next several days.

Turned out to be a good decision. While it wasn't fun, it wasn't gloomy either. Mel made up a pizza from scratch and cooked it in her BBQ on the back deck. Red wine flowed and they rehashed the day's events. It was good to get the shock out of Katie's system.

Mel phoned the hospital at 8:30 PM and spoke to a nurse she knew there.

"Good news, chickie, Big John is expected to make a full recovery. No brain damage, just a concussion. Everything else is going to heal, but he is in a lot of pain right now and his blood pressure is up there. He's medicated for that. He's going to be okay, we just need to be patient," Mel reported.

"Thank goodness. That is a relief. Wow. A huge relief. I'll drink to that."

"Cheers," Mel said.

The ladies both agreed to change topics for a while. Mel got her caught up to date on the latest listing from the morning and some of the gossip from her office.

"Did you feel the earthquake this morning?" Katie asked.

"What? What earthquake?"

"Well, maybe it was just a tremor, but it made the house shake," Katie said.

Mel pulled out her phone and did a quick search. "No earthquakes or tremors recorded anywhere near our area today," she said.

Katie looked Mel straight in the eyes. "There was at Blackstone Manor."

After a long pause, Mel said, "We need to get you out of there."

CHAPTER TWELVE

Thunderbolts pounded in Katie's head when her phone went off at 7:10 AM. A bit too much wine—again—and forgetting to put the phone on 'do not disturb' scared the wits out of her. *Who the heck would be calling me at this time in the morning?* she asked herself.

She was tempted to ignore it, but it was a good thing that she didn't. When she picked up the phone it was the security system people. She'd forgotten to turn the alarm off, and the workers who had the keys to her house had accidentally triggered it. The police were there. Not good.

The security people were nice about it. They gave you three false alarms, but because she wasn't there and the police were called she would have to pay for that call. The police were not impressed. She was terribly embarrassed when she hung up the phone.

Wide awake now, she logged into her computer to check out the security cameras. She could only imagine how frustrated the workers must've been.

She checked the library camera and sure enough they were inside working on the bookcases. It looked like one guy was getting ready to put up new wallpaper. It was hard to tell from the angle of the camera. She checked the outside cameras. Pretty cool stuff.

She clicked on the attic camera. Nothing much happening in there except the bright sunlight shining through the still dirty window. The beam of light was directed right on the mousetraps, which were still lying there in the clock formation. Katie blinked her eyes. She brought her face closer to the screen. She let out a quiet whimper and rushed to the living room carrying her laptop with her.

Mel was up and in the kitchen. She was making coffee. "Hey, chickie, how are you—"

"Am I seeing things?"

"What's up?"

Katie was shaking. She put the laptop down on the center island and was gesturing. "Look."

Mel didn't know what she was talking about. She could tell Katie was distressed and took a close look, but couldn't see anything out of the ordinary. It was just the attic.

"What was I supposed to be looking for, girlfriend?"

"The mousetraps."

"We've been through this before. There they are. They're in a circle."

"Look closer. Count them."

Mel sympathized with Katie, but was really starting to think she was losing it. Shadows, earthquakes... Even she was thinking this was getting to be a little bit too much. But she thought she would humor her anyway and took another look.

Mel's jaw went slack. She was speechless. She couldn't believe what she saw.

"Either someone is screwing with you, or something is screwing with you. But that's not funny either way."

"You see it?"

"I see it. I don't want you staying there anymore," Mel said firmly. "I'm really worried about you, and I don't want you in that house alone at any time. That is just nuts."

They both looked at the computer screen again. There, highlighted by a beam of light through the dirty old window, were the six mousetraps in a circle. But that wasn't all.

In the middle was a new trap. Right smack dead in the center.

"I'm going right over there, and I want to take those traps and I'm going to put them in a bin and set them on fire," Katie said. She was seething.

"Stop. Don't you dare. I don't want you up in that room by yourself. Do not go there. Promise?"

"I promise." Katie was shaking. "I've got Psychic Diana coming over today and I'm praying to God—if there is one—that that will put an end to all of this garbage."

Mel asked if she was going to be okay. Katie told her she would be fine, and promised to come back to the house in the evening for dinner and to sleep. Mel had to get running to work—she had a full day—and Katie wanted to have a nice long shower.

As Mel got up to go Katie remembered something from last night before she'd gone to bed. She'd been tipsy, but she remembered it clearly.

"Mel. Wait. Let me just show you one last thing quickly."

Katie opened up her email and clicked on the pictures that the man had taken of the house. Mel leaned into the screen, taking a close look as Katie magnified it by pressing some buttons.

"Tell me what you see," Katie said, pointing to the chimney and Jason standing by it.

Mel shook her head slowly. "Don't be in that house alone."

***

It was a new day, but as she rolled up to the house her feelings had totally changed about it. Yes, it was just as beautiful as it was yesterday, and to her surprise she could see the beautiful red door, which was partially open as it clearly needed to dry. But it set off the house just so perfectly.

As beautiful as it was, she hated it now. Or rather, she hated what this house represented: evil.

Katie had a new resolve. She was going to get that evil spirit out of there, even if it killed her.

The new wallpaper in the library looked magnificent even though it was only partly done. Three guys were applying stain to the old bookcases, bringing back their rich dark glory. Another young guy was placing plastic all over the fireplace in preparation for a good chimney sweep.

None of that mattered. She wanted that house gone as fast as possible. But before she could sell it, she felt an obligation to get rid of, once and for all, whatever evil was in that place.

Katie went up the stairs to the second floor. Portable spotlights were in the hallway, making it as bright as it had ever been. There was scaffolding up there, with two guys putting the finishing touches on the ceiling. It was absolutely gorgeous seeing the restored details of that ceiling, and the bright white made it seem almost heavenly.

Her phone rang, and it was Psychic Diana.

"Hey, Diana. You coming over?"

"We can be there anytime. What's best for you?"

"How does 11:30 AM sound to you? The house is full of workers, but I can send them into town for lunch while we get about doing our business."

"That sounds great. See you then." Diana hung up.

Katie went into the kitchen and sat in her favorite chair. She opened up her laptop and looked at the security cameras again. She could not take her eyes off of the traps upstairs, and she was certainly not going to go up there by herself.

There was a somber mood in the house. No music blasting from a stereo. It was natural, of course; the boys had lost a good friend of theirs and were worried about their boss.

Katie looked around the kitchen and decided there was nothing further to do at that moment in time, so she closed the laptop and decided to make a quick run out to the hospital to see how Big John was doing.

***

"I'm sorry, ma'am, he's not able to have any visitors at this moment," the nurse said.

"Pardon me. I don't mean to sound rude, but why not?"

"Are you family?"

Katie could feel a lump in her throat. This didn't sound good. "No, I'm not family, he's just a good... friend. Is there any family here right now waiting for him?"

"No, not that I'm aware of," the nurse said.

"Is he going to be okay?"

The nurse looked frustrated. She didn't have time to be chatting to somebody who wasn't family when she had other patients who needed her. But Katie was both polite and persistent—and clearly worried.

"He had a bad reaction to some drugs last night. He's in critical but stable condition. You did not hear that from me, did you?"

"Oh my God. Thank you. Would you mind letting him know that Katie came by to see him?"

"Katie? As in Katie Pearson? Are you the owner of the Blackstone house?"

"It's me. Why are you asking—"

"Come with me. He's been talking about you and asking for you nonstop. He's highly agitated, and you can help possibly calm him down. Can you help us?"

Katie was bewildered. She was being ushered to a different section of the hospital and being asked to do something she wasn't sure of. *How do you calm somebody down? I'm not a nurse. I'm not a doctor.*

"This is his room. He's on pretty strong pain medication and a little bit out of it. He's stressing that he needs to see you quickly. I need you to go in there, let him know everything is going to be okay and that you will be here for him. I need you to calm him down. I need you to tell him to listen to what we tell him to do. Understood?"

"I understand. Can I go in now?"

"Yes. Thank you for coming."

Katie slowly opened up the door. The lights were off in the hospital room except the overhead light behind him. John's leg was still propped up. He looked tucked in nicely and was seated at a 45° angle. He had an oxygen tube in his nose and was hooked up to a variety of different monitors. His eyes were closed, and the bandage was off his face. He had some pretty deep gashes that had turned into scabs. The scabs glistened with some sort of cream.

Katie touched John's left hand and his eyes slowly opened. Sure enough, his eyes were glassy from the medications. John let out a smile and said in a low voice, "Katie."

"I'm here, John. I hear you've been giving the nurses and doctors a hard time."

John let out a couple bursts of air—a laugh—it pained him, but he did find humor in it.

"John, I'm here. I need you to listen to what the doctors tell you. Everything is going great at the house. The guys are all doing well and are way ahead of schedule. There's nothing to worry about—"

John raised his hand. His eyes got larger and his face started turning slightly red. "You need to get out. Burn that place down to the ground. It will kill us all."

"It's okay, John. I'm taking care of things for sure. Whatever it is, I'm going to get rid of it."

"Do you think you are the first one to try to get rid of this? You can't. It's a phantom. A ghost. It's a black cloud of death. It attacked Jason, and it attacked me. Do you want it to attack you?"

Katie started to shake. Lovable Big John was beginning to scare her. Not in a bad way, but in a healthy way.

Katie reached into her bag and pulled out her laptop. She opened it and clicked on the photograph. She turned it and held it above John's face so he could see it.

Because the photograph was meant to capture the whole house he didn't readily recognize the chimney and Jason until she pointed them out.

John took a deep breath, his eyes widened and then suddenly the monitors started beeping loudly. "Get out of that house! Get out of that house!"

Katie was scared now. She slapped the lid of the laptop down and dropped it into the bag just as the nurse came in. "You've got to leave right now, ma'am. Please, get out right now."

Katie quickly walked out into the hallway, terrified. She waited in the hall until the nurse finally came out.

"That didn't work the way I thought. Thank you for your help," the nurse said.

"If he asks, I need you to lie to him. Tell him the house burned down and we are all okay. Hopefully that will help him."

The nurse gave Katie a weird look.

"Don't worry. It won't happen. But his head is screwed up, and if that's what it takes to calm him down, please do it."

"Thank you. I will," the nurse said. "Oh, and I will pray for you."

CHAPTER THIRTEEN

Katie laughed. Here she was sitting in the driveway of her house convincing herself that she wasn't afraid to go in. Katie had picked up an extra-large cappuccino and not one, but two pastries. *My butt needs pastries like I need a hole in the head,* she thought to herself.

She shook her head back and forth. Aren't exorcisms supposed to be done late at night under a full moon in a scary looking house?

Although overcast, it was a beautiful day. It seemed counterintuitive. She grabbed her coffee and her bag and stepped out of the car. Just then another car rolled into the front yard. It was a very old but well-kept Mercedes-Benz. Golden color. Katie stood by her car smiling, but the two passengers were in deep conversation. The woman was clearly Psychic Diana, and the gentleman was her friend.

Psychic Diana got out of the car, gave a big wave and said hello. She leaned in and mentioned something that Katie couldn't hear to the gentleman, then closed the door and enthusiastically walked up to Katie.

Katie had the giggles today. She suppressed her laugh, but Psychic Diana didn't look like any of those psychics you see on TV or read about. In fact she looked quite elegant. The woman was clearly in her 50s or so, and was wearing a beautiful purple pantsuit, a white blouse and an oversized golden necklace. Her hair was short and mostly white, but a little bit of grey remained, almost as though it was fighting the change.

"Hi, you must be Katie? I'm Diana. I'll introduce you to Frank in just a moment—he's just getting some stuff from the car and he wants to have a cigarette before he comes in. Nasty habit."

Katie was impressed. Diana could've easily been a professional businesswoman or real estate agent. She was bright, energetic and broke the mold of what you would think a psychic would look like.

"Nice to meet you, Diana. I just arrived myself. Let's head into the house. Does your friend need any help?"

"No, getting stuff out of the car is just an excuse to smoke. He will be in shortly."

The ladies walked in the front door of the house, into the great library.

"My goodness, Katie, this is an absolutely beautiful home. The outside looks absolutely incredible."

"Do you want a cup of tea or coffee?"

"No, we just did exactly as you did: we picked up our coffees on the way here. We're good to go. Tell me a little bit about what's going on."

"You want the long version or the short version?"

Diana smiled. "I need the detailed version."

Katie started to give her the story, starting with the scratching in the attic, the dreams, items being scattered. Every detail Katie could think of, she was confessing.

As she was talking, Diana walked around the library, ducking around the book-filled boxes that were on the floor. She touched bookcases with her right hand and seemed to be far off as she wandered around the room. She ended up back at the starting point and walked towards the great fireplace. It was still covered with plastic. She ran her hand along the mantle.

As Katie was speaking to her she couldn't help but think how calm she looked. She wondered what was going on inside her head. Part of Katie envied how calm Diana was knowing that this place had weird activity going on.

As Katie was sharing her story she was staring out the window and noticed the man walking slowly towards the house. He arrived at the door just as Katie was finishing off her final details of the dreams.

Katie opened the door as the man arrived.

The man looked old and frail. He stood about six-foot-two and had a balding head and a very weathered look. His clothing, unlike Diana's, was out of date. He reeked of smoke. That said, when he smiled he beamed a full set of yellowed teeth and seemed genuinely friendly.

"Hello, I'm Frank. Nice to meet you. May I come in?"

A gentleman, Katie thought. Definitely old school. He looked to be in his 80s and walked with a slight limp.

Diana let out a big smile and properly introduced them both to each other. "Katie, this is Father Frank Marlin, a retired priest who specializes in demonology. Frank, this is Katie."

"A demonologist? Oh my God. Do you think that I have demons in my house?" Katie said. She was extremely nervous.

Diana laughed. "Don't let the title scare you. It just means he specializes in exorcisms, demons, evil spirits, that sort of thing. If we find anything in the house, Father Frank is the right guy for the job."

Katie winced. That didn't exactly tell her much, and it certainly didn't do anything to calm her down. She was beginning to think that she was losing her mind. *The other day I was a nonbeliever, and now I've got a demonologist in my house. I'm losing my mind,* she thought.

Diana pulled from her bag a small leather pouch. She opened the drawstring and pulled out a crystal with a long cord attached to it. "Please give me a moment to check the energy of the house with my pendulum."

She held the cord by one end, between her thumb and first finger. Dangling down at the opposite end was the crystal, which sparkled in the sunlight. She closed her eyes and took a couple of deep breaths, and the pendulum started swinging. At first it was swinging in a straight line, and then, slowly, it started to swing in a counterclockwise circle.

"You definitely have energy in this house," she said. The pendulum kept swinging and she added, "Actually, two... three... Oh my goodness, you have six entities in this house."

Katie looked skeptical. Diane already knew this information.

Father Frank had his eyes closed and seemed to be praying. "There is definitely a heaviness in this house," he said.

Diana walked into the kitchen. She held the pendulum out, waited a moment and then placed the pendulum into her left hand. "One of the entities spends a lot of time the kitchen. The energy is very strong—"

"And the most evil," Father Frank said.

This caught Katie's attention. "Can I ask, would this energy do violent things in this room? Like move things around?"

"Absolutely," Diana said. "It's definitely very frustrated, and feels ganged up on in here. Judged. Berated. Hard to put into words, but it does not like being in this kitchen."

Katie stood silently, looking around to see if she could 'see' anything that these people were apparently seeing.

"Can we go upstairs?" Diana asked.

Katie was nervous. She gestured, "After you."

Diana slowly made her way up the stairs. Father Frank was next, but seemed to have difficulty with either his leg or his hip, managing only one step at a time. He held firmly onto the handrail with his bony hands. He was definitely over six feet tall, Katie guessed, but couldn't have weighed more than 160 pounds. He looked gaunt and not well, and his breathing sounded off. But he was determined.

"Oh my. My, my, my. I don't like this. I don't think I've ever felt energy this strong in all my life," Diana said.

"You know, that's like going to a doctor and having the doctor faint when they look at a growth on your body. You're not exactly instilling confidence in me, Diana!" Katie said. She was trying to bring some humor to the situation, but she was quite disturbed by Diana's comment. And her habit of trying to be funny in bad situations wasn't working.

Father Frank was wincing. It was hard to tell if it was because of his lowered lung capacity from coming up the stairs or from the energy he was feeling, but he now had the cross in his right hand and the bible in his left. Katie was beginning to get nervous.

"Let's begin at this end," Diana said. She headed towards the master bedroom. Her walk was determined and fearless. Katie followed after, with Father Frank walking behind. Diana stopped in the middle of the room.

"Interesting! This room is completely clear. This room was a safe place for the strongest entity."

"I'm not sure I understand. How can an evil spirit haunt a house but have a favorite place where he doesn't haunt it?" Katie asked. Her voice was agitated. She was confused.

"Spirits are no different than us. They have places that they like and feel safe in, and places that they don't like and get angry in."

Diana took an interest in the floor. "Look at that. They had two beds in this room, you can tell by the marks on the floor," she said. Diana was pointing to the faded wear marks where the bedposts rested against the wooden floor.

"They slept in separate beds. That's old school. She resents him, and is angry at him. She is constantly punishing him. He comes to bed when she's asleep and gets up before she wakes. I can feel him in here. Strangely, he feels safe because he doesn't have to interact with her, even though she's in the room with him..." Diana said. She appeared to be in some sort of trance, which fascinated Katie.

Father Frank was gripping the cross hard. So much so that she could see his knuckles turning white. It was as though he was worried something was going to jump out and attack him. This made Katie uncomfortable.

Diana's eyes suddenly closed and her voice dropped deeply. "I hate my life. I hate this house. She wants to change it. I hate it. I want to move. She wants to stay. We can afford it. I hate this house. I hate my life. I want out..."

Katie glanced at Father Frank. He was standing straight with his right arm extended and the cross pointed right towards Diana. His eyes were intense in his face, and they looked ghostly white.

Diana's eyes popped open. "Interesting." She turned abruptly and walked into the hallway.

Father Frank followed behind. It almost appeared as though he was Diana's bodyguard. In a way he was. What Katie didn't realize was that Father Frank was Diana's 'wing man.' His job was to help her if she got into trouble. He didn't say it out loud, but he too had never experienced energy anywhere else that was as strong as this.

Diana stopped dead in her tracks only steps outside the door. "Hello. Who might you be?"

Diana was looking straight ahead towards the other end of the hall outside of the unfinished bedroom. Katie couldn't see anything, but to be fair she was blocked by Frank and Diana. It struck Katie that it might be a good idea to perhaps take some pictures. She reached into her back pocket and pulled out her phone, then turned it on and waited.

"And what is your name, son?" Diana was asking an empty hallway.

Diana stood in the hallway for a moment. Katie couldn't see it, but her eyes were closed. The person she was connecting with was not visible to the naked eye. But Diana could see him in the theater of her own mind.

Diana stopped, turned around and said to Frank and Katie, "There is a young man in this hallway by the name of Daniel. He's very protective of his two sisters. I believe he's the middle boy. And–"

Diana turned back again towards the other end of the hallway. Katie couldn't see anything, but it seemed like she was having a conversation with somebody behind her.

Diana started to laugh. "Bootleggers. Many years ago the family were bootleggers. There are secret doors and sliding panels in this house, he says."

Katie said nothing. She tried her best to keep a poker face, and she didn't want to tell the psychic about the hidden cubbyhole in that room.

Diana turned towards the wall with a look of great fascination. She leaned down and started knocking on the wood paneling. At one part she placed her palm flat against the wood and pushed.

Father Frank gave her a quizzical look, as did Katie. But all were surprised when the panel pushed in about two inches. She wiggled her hand slightly and all three were surprised when the panel slid open to reveal a very small, compact space.

"My goodness, the boy's right. There's a small cask of booze sitting in there."

Father Frank bent his gangly frame over and peered in. "Jesus!"

Diana laughed. Katie move forward and was shocked to see a cask inside this hidden compartment.

If this was some sort of elaborate hoax, it was a good one. There was no way anybody could have known about that hidden panel, and if they did they probably would've taken that cask out to look into it. It was completely covered in thick dust and there were no signs of anything having been in there in a long, long time. Katie was stunned.

"We are not allowed to go upstairs," Diana said. "Daniel's father has forbidden them from going upstairs."

Father Frank looked directly into Diana's eyes and paused. Diana nodded her head, as though she could read his mind. Diana turned, and headed up the staircase.

"Wait. That's where the weird stuff happens with the mousetraps," Katie said. Her voice betrayed her fear.

Father Frank turned to her. He looked afraid, yet calmly said, "Yes. And that's exactly why we must go there."

CHAPTER FOURTEEN

"Oh," was all Diana said. She stood at the top of the stairs looking at the door. She was frozen.

All of them froze as the door seemed to be moving on its own. At first, Katie strained her eyes. The staircase was dark, so seeing things easily wasn't going to happen. At first glance, it looked like a breeze was moving the door in and out slightly in its frame. Only the door was locked. Sure, there might have been a bit of give in the old frame, but not like this.

No. The door appeared to be... breathing.

Father Frank held the cross up towards the door, mumbling something under his breath. He startled Diana and Katie by blurting out, "Back away, Satan!"

The door returned to normal, but not without a large and heavy knock, as though someone had banged it in protest.

Diana turned to Frank. He nodded and she turned back and grabbed the doorknob. Suddenly, she yanked her hand back.

"It's hot!"

She quickly pulled her jacket sleeve over her left hand and deftly grabbed the handle and gave it a fast twist and push, causing the door to swing open. They were all blinded by the light of the room.

Diana slowly walked in. For a brief moment, Katie admired her bravery. She wondered about Frank, though. He seemed to be only dragging along.

As Katie was the last to step into the room, she touched the doorknob with her hand, partly in skepticism. It was very warm. Unusually warm. Her heart was pounding and her palms were clammy.

"The traps are still—"

The six mousetraps that lay in the center of the room suddenly flew across the floor in all directions—startlingly fast—as though the center trap had become a reverse-polarity magnet. The trap which was at the six o'clock position furiously slid across the floor, hitting Father Frank's foot before he could hop out of the way.

Father Frank furiously threw his right hand containing the cross toward the center of the room. "In the name of the Father, the Son and the Holy Spirit, I rebuke you! You shall not have power over us!"

Katie dropped her phone and stood with her back against the wall nearest the door. Her heart was pounding like a freight train. Her left hand clawed into the wall behind her. All three were back against the wall, staring into the center of the empty attic.

Katie glanced down and looked at her phone. She did a double-take when she noticed it was in camera mode and she saw something. Squatting down, she deftly grabbed it and slid with her back to an upright position as she held the phone in front of her.

She glanced at the screen. The picture was taken at a 45° angle but was clear. She must have accidentally pressed the camera button when she was walking into the room. There, in the photo, were the six traps neatly arranged, and hovering above them was a large black orb.

The orb wasn't perfectly formed. It looked more like a circular cloud of smoke. The muscles in her face weakened and her jaw hung open. She quickly glanced up and could see nothing.

Diana was breathing rapidly. Her eyes closed, she began talking. It didn't make sense at first but quickly became clear.

"Mother. Mother. Ma... she lives here. Not well, quite ill. Angry. Jealous. Bitter..."

Father Frank was mumbling prayers in such a way that Katie was having a hard time hearing what Diana was saying. She leaned in and strained to focus.

"The origin of the evil. Angry with Johnny. Angry. Johnny has failed. You are a failure, Johnny. We lived like royalty, Johnny, and now you are bringing us all down..." Diana said. She was talking softer and softer, in a higher pitched voice. Diana's face was getting redder, and then it tightened.

"Bastard! You bastard! You can't do anything right! You are an embarrassment to the family, to your family, to your children... I wish you were never born!"

Diana had separated herself from the wall and moved two steps towards the center of the room. Father Frank was still against the wall, with his right hand extended and his bible held up to his forehead, praying in a mumbled fashion.

For some inexplicable reason—still filled with fear—Katie wondered if her camera could catch another orb pic. Taking a deep breath she raised up her phone and closed her eyes, taking a pic. She opened her eyes and looked at the camera.

"Oh my God!" Katie blurted out. Diana and Frank didn't hear her fearful comment. She looked again at the camera and now, in the middle of the room, was a massive black orb. Or cloud. Or evil thing. Whatever it was, it was huge and terrifying.

"Her anger is now in John. John has been possessed by her evil ways. She is practicing black magic! Dear God, she's put a curse on Johnny and the house... she wants us all... dead!"

Father Frank was shaking. Mumbling prayers. His right hand started shaking violently.

"Death to all who dare take this house from me!" Diana screamed. Tears were streaming down her face. "You have taken from me! I will take from you all!"

Father Frank stepped forward. Diana opened her eyes and grabbed his left arm. "Be careful Frank!" He pulled away from her abruptly. She made the sign of the cross.

A horrid smell filled the room. It smelled of death. Rotting flesh.

Diana stepped back and with her right arm grabbed Katie's left forearm. "Don't move. We are protected by God's white light."

It felt as though their feet were tingling. A tingling sensation that quickly changed to a shaking vibration.

"Earthquake," Katie squealed.

The house started shaking more. It felt as though the house was being dragged down a staircase. Sounds of banging, thuds and groans were heard.

"In the name of the Father, the Son and the Holy Spirit, I rebuke you and cast you out of this home. I rebuke you, Satan, and order you to leave immediately," Father Frank said. His words were staccato, wheezing in manner. He was shaking hard.

Katie glanced at Diana and could see terror in her face. Her eyes were closed, but what she was seeing? It wasn't good.

"Diana. Diana. What's going on?"

"Pray. Pray. We need to pray. Quickly!"

Katie prayed as best she could, "God, please help us get rid of this evil from the house. Please, God. Please..."

Father Frank had his back to the women and was now in the center of the room. His body was shaking visibly from head to toe as he prayed loudly. He suddenly thrust his arms up in the air, his bible in his left hand and his silver cross in his right.

At that moment a blinding flash of white light appeared and then just as suddenly vanished. It was as though someone had shone a massive searchlight through the window and then turned it off. So bright, it made Katie momentarily blind.

Katie's heart was pounding violently. She tried to open her eyes, but the blindness was still subsiding.

Diana had her right hand clamped to Katie's left forearm so much it actually hurt.

"You okay, Diana?"

"Yes. Yes. I'm good. I think... Frank? Are you okay?"

Katie's vision was returning. Frank was slowly lowering his arms back to his sides.

"It worked, Frank! You've cast out the demon! Great job, Fr—"

Frank dropped both his bible and cross and slowly slumped to the floor. He reached up with his right arm and grasped his chest.

"FRANK!" Diana screamed. "Call 911, Katie!"

***

"How much have you had to drink?" Mel demanded.

"I just opened up my second bottle. Do you want some?"

Mel poured herself a glass and ushered Katie into the living room. "What the hell happened? I dropped in to see

Diana on the way home and she's an absolute basket case."

"All hell broke loose," Katie said. Then she burst out laughing. *All hell broke loose, I'll say,* she thought. "You told me to bring them in, I did, and it turns out that Casper is not a very friendly ghost after all," she said.

"Go on."

"Apparently the house is a portal to her. Mother, that is. She poisoned her son. She's gone completely bonkers, and apparently drove him bonkers to. The only place he can hang out is in my bedroom. She promised to kill everybody that came in contact with the house. Do I have to disclose that if I sell it to somebody?"

Katie was slurring her words, trying to be funny.

"You can't go back there. We'll figure something out, but you can't go back there."

"This better not be a prank. Because it's not funny. I'm not laughing."

"It's not a joke."

"I wonder how Frank is doing..."

Mel paused and looked out the massive windows over-looking the beautiful lake. "He, uh, well, he didn't make it, Katie."

Katie got up and calmly walked to the kitchen. She popped open another bottle of wine, poured another glass and returned to the living room, bringing the bottle with her.

Neither woman said a word. Both faced the window and stared for what seemed like eternity.

Then the tears came. A storm of emotions burst out of Katie. She was sobbing uncontrollably, so much so that she had to put her glass of wine down.

Mel got up and sat beside her and gave her a big hug. "It's going to be okay, chickie. We'll figure this out."

"I watched him die, Mel. I watched that thing get him and kill him—"

Katie suddenly stood up and went back to the kitchen where she had dropped her purse and keys. She pulled out her phone and hurried back to the living room. "Here, look."

Mel took her phone and looked at the screen. She looked at the hallway picture and noticed an orb. She flicked through to the picture in the attic. "Holy crap."

"Heh heh," Katie laughed out loud and swigged another gulp of red wine. "Wait for it. Wait for it..."

Mel flicked to the next picture. She sat stunned. She was looking at it just like people do when they pass a car crash: you know you shouldn't stare, but you do anyway.

"What is it?"

"Beats me. Your buddy talked to it. It killed Father Frank. I'm guessing it's not very friendly..." Katie said. Her slurring was getting slightly more pronounced.

"But is it gone?"

"I hope so. I want to finish the house up and dump it. Quick."

"Katie. Listen, I'm not letting you go back. Not unless we are sure that this... thing... is gone."

"Uh, it's apparently a double-thing. Evil mother apparently drove son nutty. I think the evil thing is him, with her inside... or... something like that."

"Double evil? Sounds like the poor guy had an abusive mother. Stories were told of her living quite the socialite life when she was younger. Then she got older and got sick. Sounds like she got bitter."

"Was there an earthquake today? Wait. Don't tell me. No, right?" Katie asked.

Mel considered cutting Katie off from drinking, but after what she'd gone through today and the past while, she figured she needed the medication. As it turned out, Katie fell asleep on the couch in short order.

CHAPTER FIFTEEN

Hangovers suck, Katie thought, struggling to get out of Mel's comfortable guest bed. She stretched, held her forehead and meandered to the kitchen.

Wow. Bright.

Coffee was brewed and waiting. A note from Mel said just one thing: "Call me."

Grabbing the coffee, she headed to the shower. The heat and the steam was glorious and revitalizing. Yesterday seemed a thousand miles away. The shower was like the safety of a womb.

Katie toweled off and got dressed. The pills were kicking in and the headache was slowly ebbing. Katie headed back to the couch and looked out over the beautiful lake. *Wish I lived here.*

"Hey, chickie. How's the head?"

"Getting better. Wow, though. I don't even remember going to bed."

"Well. You decided to take off your clothes in the living room and I had to bribe you to your bedroom with a glass of wine."

Katie winced. "That bad, huh?"

"It was a bad day, Katie."

"Where are you?"

Mel paused. "I'm actually at your house. You were out cold this morning and I knew that your contractors would be here, so I came to get them going—"

"I'll be right over—"

"NO! I've got it. Really, I don't think you should be here for a wee bit, and I definitely don't think you should ever be here alone."

"I've survived so far—"

"Katie. No. At least maybe not for the next couple of days. Listen, I'll be home shortly, I've got some lunch for us and we'll talk more. The guys are working away here, and everything is fine, so you don't need to be here."

Katie paused. Maybe Mel was the voice of reason. Maybe a couple days off would be in order. Her stress level must be pushing her blood pressure off the charts. Reluctantly, Katie agreed and Mel promised to be home within an hour.

***

"Miss Pearson? This is Stan. I'm one of the wallpaper contractors. Good news: The library is looking amazing, but we have questions about how to paper around the fireplace. We need to run this by you because Big John isn't here to answer for us—"

Katie looked at the time. Mel was supposed to have been home long ago.

"Hey, Stan, can I speak to Mel?"

"She left hours ago."

"Are you sure?"

"Yes, I saw her drive away."

"Okay. Um. Let me call you right back."

Katie hung up the phone and then immediately dialed Mel. Mel's phone went to voicemail. She hung up and then called Mel's office. Ingrid answered and told Katie that Mel hadn't been in all day.

It was unlike Mel to be late. She was always on time or had the decency to call. Katie began to panic.

"Hey, Stan, I'm coming over now. If Mel shows up, have her call me immediately, please... no problem, I will see you soon."

Katie hopped in her car and headed to the house. She called Mel and left a message. "Mel. Where are you? I'm worried. Call me back right away on my cell."

***

Driving up the long, windy road gave Katie the heebie-jeebies. The only consolation was that Mel wasn't at the house.

As Katie got out of her car, hatred filled her heart. A hatred she'd never felt before in her life. "Oh my God, has this... demon... gotten a hold of me?" she said out loud. She felt like she wanted to hurt something. It was a horrible feeling.

Katie pushed open the door and found four men sitting in the living room. Up jumped one man, almost embarrassed for being caught sitting on the job.

"Hello, I'm Stan!"

"Hey, Stan," she said, trying to muster reasonable enthusiasm. "This room looks magnificent. You've done a great job. Big John will be proud."

"Oh," he paused, glancing a nervous look to the other men, who'd frozen up at the mention of Big John's name.

Katie looked at the men. Then back to Stan. She stepped toward him with a murderous look. "What happened? Spit it out."

Stan leaned back from the intenseness of Katie's demeanor. He didn't mince his words: "Big John had a massive stroke this morning. Not sure if he'll make it."

Katie stood in place, closed her eyes and took in a deep breath. *Stay calm. Stay. Calm.*

Nobody moved or said a word. All eyes were on Katie. She opened her eyes and coolly asked, "What was your question for me?"

There was argument amongst the men about where to stop and start the wallpaper around the intricate design of the fireplace. Katie told them what she wanted, asked if there was anything else and then left quietly, dialing Mel as she walked out the door.

The door closed behind her, and looking out Katie was startled to see Chris Watkin standing by the willow tree. Anger surged through her. Her eyes felt burning warm and it felt like hate was burning through her bloodstream.

"The house looks... majestic... I love what you have—"

"Shut up. What the hell lived—or lives—in this... this..." Katie stuttered, at a loss for words.

"I don't understand?"

"This is a hell-hole you sold me. It's a house of death and horrors—"

Christopher's left eye twitched. He was staring at Katie in disbelief and relief at the same time. "You've seen it?"

"Yes! Yes I have. And I'm not the only one—"

"Wait. You saw the specter?"

"What the hell is a specter? A ghost? A cloud? Darkness? Whatever the hell you call it? YES, damn it, I've got a freaking picture of it!"

Christopher's face went blank. "Everyone thought I was crazy. My wife said she saw it. I swear it killed her... nobody believed me. Nobody..."

This wasn't what Katie had expected. Her anger softened slightly. "Where did you feel it or experience it, Chris? Tell me!"

"Upstairs. As soon as we would leave the bedroom, it would get... depressing. I'd hear noises in the attic, that's where Blackstone's mother was murdered. There was nothing in there, but wow, it made me want to be sick..." Chris drifted back to a memory from long ago.

"I need you to go on, Chris. What else?"

Christopher was staring at the house. "Children. I'd hear children. We never had children, and it was torture to hear, my wife wanted kids so badly..."

"Go on. I need to hear about everything, Chris."

"The kitchen was my favorite place to sit. Bright, airy. Felt good. But, I wanted to..."

"Chris. What did you want?"

"I wanted to kill someone. At first, it was me. Then, I thought of killing... anyone," he said. Then he glanced at Katie.

"No, no I didn't act on it. It was a horrible feeling. Horrible. So I locked the house up. I often come by to check on it. Sorry to spook you—"

"Chris, is the bedroom safe?"

"Yes. Nothing ever happens there. It's peaceful in there. The only problem is that you have to walk through the house to get to it, or leave."

"Thanks. Thanks for coming by. Thanks for checking in, Chris."

***

Katie pulled into a roadside diner. She placed another call to Mel with no luck. Another call to the office. Hadn't seen her all day.

Katie called the hospital. She braced herself for bad news, but was partially relieved to hear that John was in serious but stable condition.

The open faced hot turkey sandwich was barely pass-able, the coffee the most horrid she had had in a long time. Thankfully, she got talked into a lemon merengue pie that was not only delicious, but fresh. Something good was happening today. She slid a bite between her lips and let it melt in her mouth.

The monitors, she thought. The thought came out of nowhere. Katie pulled out her laptop and logged into her security system. It took a few minutes to figure out, but she replayed the attic footage. Minutes ticked by. "Come on," she said out loud.

Nearly ten minutes had passed when she hit the right spot. All three of them in the attic. Against the wall. It looked funny watching it fast-forward. Frank looked terri-fied looking at him from the side. No shadow could be seen.

"Wait," Katie said, to nobody. She darted her eyes from side to side to see if anyone had caught her talking to herself.

She rewound the recording to prior to them entering.

"No mousetraps? How can that be?"

She fast forwarded the video to where they were against the wall and Father Frank was moving forward. There he was, raising his bible and cross and then...

The camera went white. Katie hit rewind and played it again. It was a recording glitch. After 32 seconds the recording was back and Diana was standing over Father Frank, who was lying on his back.

Had Father Frank given his life to save them? To save her?

Could the evil bastard be gone?

Katie wanted to find Mel. She picked up her phone, but the moment the screen turned on, it went off. Battery was dead. Damn it.

Logging into her email she sent Mel a message: "Where are you? What happened to you? You vanished. I'm heading to the house—call me crazy—but I need to check some things out. Big John stable, but not good. Love you, KP. Oh. LOL. BTW, Chris showed up today. He described the entity to a T. Seemed relieved I experienced it too. Xoxo

Closing her laptop, she left cash on the counter and headed back to the house.

***

The sun had nearly set. Stan was packing his van and was the only one left.

"Hey, Miss Pearson. Running a bit late, but I'll be out of your way in about five minutes."

"No problem." She walked into the library, fully lit, wallpapered and with a crackling fire. "Did they chimney sweep today?"

"Yes. The contractor disconnected an old bad electric wire on the chimney and they swept as well. The guy said it is a miracle this place didn't burn down 50 years ago."

"Wow. I burned a few fires—"

"Dear God. I've never seen so much crap come out of a chimney before! You're lucky to be alive—"

Katie laughed sarcastically. "Yeah. In more ways than you know."

The wallpapering looked stunning, particularly around the fireplace. The bookcases were back to their magnificent glory, just awaiting books to be put back. Someone had put a small number of books back on a shelf to show what it would look like.

"You didn't see Mel, did you?"

"Not since this morning. Just us workers today, we'd remember pretty ladies. Good night."

Katie smiled at the creepy comment. *What is it with contractors hitting on clients?* She laughed. She stood on the porch as Stan drove away. Taking a deep breath, she turned and walked back in.

The library looked stunning. The house actually looked warm and inviting. Still, she was as nervous and as trusting as a frightened cat. One move—just one move—and she'd be gone.

With her car keys in her pocket, she latched the front door, walked to the kitchen and turned on the lights. She scurried back to the fireplace. *Jesus, stop being so jittery!*

Reaching down to her bag, she pulled out her laptop, cords and phone. She immediately plugged her phone in and hooked up to the internet. She set the alarms in the house and also set the motion detectors to beep if there was any movement.

Sure enough, she stood up and 'beeeeeep' went the alarm. Loud, too. If something was coming to get her, it would startle both her and it. "Boo!" she said out loud, then laughed.

A bit relaxed now, she made a pot of green tea. She poured it into a super-sized novelty cup, one that could hold about four normal sized mugs, and headed upstairs. She left all the lights on.

Amazingly, she had forgotten about the sliding panel in the hallway, which was still open. But it was a bit too dark up there to be peeking into, so decided to leave it for another day. *Whatever is in there has been there for fifty years, another few days won't hurt anything.*

Walking into her bedroom she looked around. It was normal. "Clear," according to Diana. She closed the door to the bedroom and slid a chair up against it. *Overkill,* she thought, but it was going to be one day at a time to heal from the stuff she had gone through these past few days.

Her dad used to tell her to watch cartoons when she was sad or sick. Laughter heals, he'd told her. So, lying in bed, she surfed online to find some of her favorite comedians. She watched old Tommy Cooper skits, but not even he could make her smile. It was just too much. She closed her laptop and rolled over.

I'll never fall asleep, she thought. Famous last words.

CHAPTER SIXTEEN

Katie woke up. For the first time in a long time she hadn't had that awful nightmare. The curtains were closed, her room was dark and she could see the nightlight on in the hallway. For once, everything seemed to be good.

She rolled onto her side facing the door. She closed her eyes, took in a deep breath and prepared to go back to sleep again.

But something wasn't right. She couldn't put her finger on it, but something wasn't right. Maybe she was supposed to have a nightmare? Maybe that was it. She opened up her eyes and looked in the hallway again. The nightlight seemed awfully bright. Was that her imagination? Probably.

She closed her eyes again. But that niggling, annoying, feeling you get when you just know that something isn't right was beginning to frustrate her.

Might as well get up and have a pee and check things out, she thought to herself. She slowly rolled out of bed, stood up and walked down the hall. A light was coming from downstairs.

Did I leave the light on in the kitchen? The library? That's weird, she thought. She headed downstairs. It wasn't her imagination: The kitchen light was still on. As she turned the corner to the kitchen in preparation to turn the light switch off, she froze.

There was an older man sitting in 'her chair' at the kitchen table. He was slightly balding, wearing a white shirt, with his elbows on the table and his hands in the prayer position. His head was pressed against his hands and his eyes closed.

Katie stood frozen. Her mind started racing: Is this guy a vagrant? Did you break in for food? What is he here for?

He appeared not to have heard her turn the corner, and she stood there frozen in fear that he might notice her. He was speaking extremely softly, as in prayer.

On the table before him were the old black bible and a beautiful wooden box. On the top of the box lay glasses. The man slowly sat upright and slowly opened up his eyes... Then he froze. He was staring right at Katie.

Katie was absolutely paralyzed in fear. The man looked dumbstruck.

"Hello," he said very softly. His face was devoid of any emotion. He looked tired and beaten by life.

Katie's whole body tightened. She was frozen there like a statue without a clue what to do. The first thought that ran through her mind was, *What the hell were you thinking coming down here unarmed?* She found herself shocked when she uttered the word "hello" back.

The man looked even more stunned. He slid his elbows off the table but kept his hands clasped together in a prayer position, resting them on the edge of the table. His shirt was white and unbuttoned down to his collar, and his sleeves were rolled up to his elbows. The shirt was clean, but clearly not new. He had sweat stains underneath his arms.

"You can see me, can't you?" the man said.

"Who are you?" Katie asked. She was utterly terrified, but for some strange reason felt comfortable enough to get some information from this intruder. Only, he seemed familiar.

The man continued to look puzzled. As though that was one of the weirdest questions in the world to ask.

He paused, then said, "I'm John. Are you... an angel?"

Okay. This guy is nuts. And crazy people do crazy things. Tread carefully, girl, Katie thought.

"Sit. Sit. Please, how rude of me. Please. Sit right here," he said. He gestured to the seat across from him.

Katie decided it was best if she listened to what he asked. She slowly eased into the chair, keeping its back to her left side. Instinctively, she felt that if this guy were to lunge at her she could lean backwards and possibly escape. But she couldn't help the overwhelming feeling that he just wanted to talk. He didn't seem to want to hurt her. But she was going to play it safe.

"Sorry. Are you John Blackstone?" she asked. The question seemed to be a stupid one, though, especially given that he wouldn't have been able to live this long.

While his demeanor remained calm, his face twisted slightly in puzzlement at the question. "Of course."

Both remained calm and quiet for a moment. Katie slowly took her eyes off of John and looked at the clock on the wall which was ticking away loudly. Weird, as she didn't have a clock on the wall. She looked back to John. John was staring back at her blankly.

"I have prayed to you and begged and pleaded for mercy. And yet you have found it in your heart to ignore me. I have been faithful to you in every way, done all I can for my family, and you have forsaken me. Please, tell me why?"

Good God. This guy thinks I'm an angel. What do I do now? Katie thought to herself.

As the fear started to build up in Katie, a plate smashed in the sink. She jumped slightly and let out a gasp. A woman in a dress, wearing an apron, was standing at the sink.

"You've ruined my life, John. You've ruined all of our lives. The children are devils and you put all this burden on me. You have shamed me, John. You shamed me, the children, and your mother!" The woman was shouting.

John put his elbows back on the table. His hands were still in the classic prayer position. He meekly mumbled, "You stopped going to church, Agnes, and so have the children—"

"There's more to life than just the church, John. I'm tired of the judgment, I'm tired of their backstabbing, I'm tired of the gossip. The Reverend only wants money, money, money—"

John slammed his right palm down on the table with a surprisingly loud bang. He turned to his wife. "We must go to church or God will punish us!"

Katie turned to the kitchen sink, but the woman—Agnes, apparently—was gone.

Good God. I'm actually inside this guy's mind. I'm hearing his... thoughts. I'm in this guy's head... I'm not in danger... Oh my God, his family is... Oh my God-

John sat still, with his eyes closed, taking slow, deep breaths. His face was expressionless. Katie gazed out the kitchen windows, but there was nothing but a white haze, like a movie screen waiting for something to project onto it.

There was no sound. The kitchen seemed... brighter, even whiter than she recalled. The black and white tiles were spotless. It was as though she was in a television studio, where they make an exact replica of something... like the Oval Office in the White House... but this was her kitchen...

"There's not much time. There's not much time left," John said. He was growing ever so slightly agitated.

Katie glanced at the clock—the clock that hadn't been on the wall but was now—and the time was 3:35. She looked at John, who was mumbling something that she couldn't make out...

Wait. Holy crap. 4:44 and 3:35... Oh my God, I've only got nine minutes with this guy...

If Katie's calculations were correct, she would wake up in a few moments. Assuming she was dreaming. If she wasn't dreaming, then she had an ominous feeling that something bad was going to happen. Either way, she was witnessing a nightmare.

Think fast. Compose yourself. He thinks you are an angel. Talk to him calmly. But be quick, you don't have much time.

Katie adjusted herself as John was praying and holding his bible. He kept kissing the cover.

"Hey, John? Where are the kids right now?"

John had the bible in his right hand resting on the table, and with his left hand he was absentmindedly stroking the wooden box. "They are at school," he said. He added, "My wife is out running errands."

"John, doesn't your mother live with you?"

John squirmed in his chair. He clearly didn't like that question. His mouth tightened and his eyes became beady. He shifted slightly in his chair and squeezed his bible tighter. "She's upstairs in her suite. Sleeping... Oh Lord. Forgive me Lord. Have mercy on your servant..."

"John, I'm here. I'm listening. Share with me your troubles... of your heart," Katie said awkwardly. She was trying to sound religious, wondering what angels would talk like.

John's voice started to crack. He shook his head slightly.

"It's too late. They've... they've gone too far to be pleasing to the Lord," John said. He let out a loud sob which startled both him and Katie. He quickly fought it back and regained his composure.

Katie glanced at the wall. Time was ticking by. It was 3:38 PM.

"It's never too late, John. What do you feel they have —"

John slammed his bible down on the table with greater force than before. Katie's eyes were wide with fear and adrenaline and the room seemed to fade.

No, no, no! I don't want to wake up yet, she thought. Her demand seemed to work, as the light volume seemed to get much brighter—almost blindingly white—and then returned. She was startled somewhat to see John leaning in on the table berating her.

"Elizabeth is just like her mother. She no longer attends church. She was such a good, good girl when she was young. Now she is under the influence of Agnes—"

"She's young, John—"

"None of that! I'll have nothing to do with that! She has a boyfriend and she smokes. In public. Disgusting. Filthy!" he hissed.

"I've prayed and I've prayed. I've worked hard, but God has not seen fit to honor my prayers. I know what he wants me to do...

"Daniel, he was a good boy and looked after his sister. But he doesn't respect me or his mother. At all. No re-

152 · JAMES M. MATHESON

spect. He must respect authority. His mother has poisoned him. He's on the wrong path," John said. He sobbed again.

"Agnes has a disease. She got it through inappropriate relations with a man before she met me. She hid it from me. Now it's eating her brain... she's drinking booze constantly, she's a drunk. A lush. An embarrassment..."

John paused. His mind was running wildly as he confessed. Katie was wondering what else to say to encourage him more, but before she could speak, he continued on. His tone was darker.

"The pastor has been of no help or guidance. God has not answered my prayers. I have been faithful. But God has given me this evil woman and disrespectful children. No answers. No answers..."

John struggled with his thoughts. Katie looked at the clock. *Good God, it's 3:40, come on man, talk! Spit it out!*

John let out another loud sob. "I lost my job at the sawmill. Two weeks ago. Too many managers. I was the best one. The best, but they gave me my papers. Oh God," he sobbed. He wiped his left eye with his hand, quickly returning it to the box.

"The bank wants the house back? Over my dead body. Greedy, evil men. Kick you when you are down."

"It's all in my hands now. I have to save my family from embarrassment, ridicule and shame. Shame, shame, shame."

"Whoa, John. We must all walk our own paths," Katie said, again feeling stupid for trying to sound religious. But it sounded good. "God is pleased with you, John."

"NO!" John shouted. "No, if He were pleased I would not be made to suffer like this. I must wipe the slate clean."

As John spoke he slowly opened the beautiful wooden box. The lid was hinged, and as he opened the box the lid lifted up and swung towards Katie, resting on the table. The interior was velvet. He removed a black silk cloth covering the object within. Katie winced as she saw the revolver.

John removed the revolver with reverence. Katie knew nothing of guns, but this was clearly an old revolver like she'd seen in old westerns. John picked out shells and started sliding them into the revolver chambers one by one. He was slow and methodical.

"I have done all that I can do. What else can I do? I speak with the authority of a husband over his wife and children, and they don't obey. I pray, I get no answer or help...

"I cannot allow this to continue. I must discipline them and put them on the right path. They must be saved..."

Katie's stomach turned. She was watching a rerun of a movie where she knew the outcome. She was powerless to stop what was happening. Anger and rage at his attitude tore through her soul. *This guy is nuts,* she thought.

The time was now 3:43. Katie felt desperate. Helpless. Sick. She wanted to run, but couldn't.

"John, you don't have to do this," she said. She tried to be calm, but she could hear the fear in her own voice.

"Thank you for being here. I had faith angels would come to comfort me," John said. His composure was back. He was sitting calmly again. He reached over, slowly, and closed the beautiful wooden box. He was holding the gun in his left hand and picked up his bible in his right.

"God is good. God is great. I love the Lord with all my —"

Noise and activity came from outside the front door. Someone had arrived. Actually, it sounded like several people had arrived.

"It is time. Please excuse me," John said.

It was 4:44 PM

CHAPTER SEVENTEEN

The front door burst open with Adelle beaming. "Daddy!" she called out enthusiastically. She ran to him and gave him a leg hug by the fireplace.

She was quickly followed by Daniel. "Hi, Dad, you are home early!" He took Adelle's hand and led her to the kitchen.

Agnes followed, carrying groceries. "What are you home for? You need to teach Danny to pull up his socks and help with these damn things, John," she said.

A cursing woman? You despicable and disrespectful woman, John thought. She knew just the right thing to say at just the right time to set him off. If there was ever a sign that he was on the right path, it was this.

"Daniel! Take your sister upstairs," John said. His voice was firm and disciplined. He meant business.

Daniel knew that voice. It meant trouble. It meant Mom was in trouble for being tipsy again and a lot of shouting and bible verses were about to fly. He grabbed his sister, who was terrified of 'that voice that Daddy makes.' They rushed up the stairs.

It wasn't the first time John had raised his voice. Agnes knew what was coming. She loved it. She loved getting John mad. It made her feel like she had power over his obsessive and controlling nature. His way or no way.

"The fire is nearly out. You can't even get a fire started properly, John. You make me sick, do you hear me—"

"I lost my job. They gave me my walking papers, Agnes."

Agnes was stunned. The air hung thick with an awkward silence. "Oh my God, what are we going to do?"

Agnes's eyes began to well up. The first emotion she had shown in ages. Tipsy from alcohol, she lowered her head into her hands.

John let out a sob. He reached out with his left hand, keeping his right hand behind his back. *A breakthrough with Agnes? Is this the healing that the angel hinted at?*

Agnes slowly turned and started to move away towards the center of the library.

I guess not, John thought.

John raised his gun and shot her point blank in the back of the head. Agnes dropped quickly face-forward with a loud thud onto the floor.

Katie was frozen in shock as she stood in the kitchen doorway. She watched in horror as John calmly lowered the gun to his side and stepped forward to look at Agnes.

John took a deep, deep breath and let out a loud sigh. "You shall sin no more, my beloved. In the name of the Father, the Son and the Holy Spirit, I give you back to God..."

A feeling of pure evil seemed to permeate the air. It was like the air was thinner and hard to breathe. From the corner of her eye she saw Daniel at the top of the stairs. He was staring right at her.

"Come quick! Dad is angry, come on!" Daniel said. He was pleading with Katie to come up the stairs. "Run!"

Katie was gasping for air. Now she was pleading to wake up! She didn't want to see any more.

Katie turned towards John, who was kneeling by Agnes. His head was down and he was checking to see if she was truly dead. She was. He raised his head and looked at the stairs. His eyes were bloodshot red.

John growled. "I said take your sister upstairs!"

"Run!" Daniel pleaded. Katie realized he was pleading to her.

Katie turned and started up the stairs, tripping on the third step. She pulled herself up, grabbing the handrail on the right. She looked around the corner and Daniel had a look of utter terror in his eyes. Katie scrambled and got up, only to have her right foot yanked hard.

Instinctively, Katie kicked hard in a backwards direction. Whatever had grabbed her leg let go, but pain seared her ankle. She ran as fast as she had ever run in her life.

Daniel was by the empty bedroom when she got to the top of the stairs. He ducked in with a motion to follow him quickly.

Katie ran in and slapped the door with her hand. The door slammed shut. *Not the brightest thing to do when trying to hide. Too late. It's done.*

Daniel was standing by the wall. Katie was amazed to see that there was a large opening in the wall. A hidden cubby hole. Inside was Adelle, terrified. Daniel's eyes were wide as he franticly pointed to get in.

"Get in here. Quick, before he comes!"

Katie slid in as fast as she could, knocking Adelle accidentally. Adelle immediately hugged Katie.

"Stay here," Daniel said. He started sliding the hidden panel back into place.

"Wait! Get in here!"

"Not enough room. It's okay. I always take the beatings. I love you, Addy," Daniel said.

Daniel slammed the sliding panel shut. Sudden blackness. Adelle squeezed her harder and was whimpering.

"Shh. We have to be quiet, okay?"

Katie could hear Daniel move to the other side of the room. She could only guess what he was doing. The room was empty; there was no place to hide. She hoped he was behind the door, but John was a big man and could easily overcome anything his son could hope to try.

A feeble muffled voice broke the silence. "John? Johnny? What was that noise?"

"Nothing, Mother. I dropped something. Dinner will be soon. I will bring it up for you."

"Johnny. I want to know what that noise was! Answer me. Do you hear me? Johnny. Answer me."

The sound of footsteps slowly trod up two flights of stairs to his mother Ellen's room in the attic. A few moments of silence followed. Then a gunshot and another dull thud.

Adelle cried softly, "Daddy is mad."

"Shhh. We have to be quiet."

It was probably only seconds, but it seemed like hours. Nothing in the house made a sound. When the silence did break, it came from an unexpected source.

"I'm home," came a voice from downstairs. The door slammed. Then the voice screamed, "MOM!"

Footsteps thundered across the floor upstairs, a door banged and the pace of the thundering continued down the stairs. John was going to shoot Elizabeth.

Suddenly the bedroom door was heard to swing open. Daniel screamed, "Run, Elizabeth, RUN!"

The thundering footsteps stopped dead in their tracks.

"Are you okay? Where are you?" Elizabeth called out.

"RUN, Lizzie, Ru—"

A loud shot rang out. "Daddy. Please. No. Nooo."

Another shot fired. Adelle buried her face into Katie's chest.

The footsteps calmly climbed the stairs and paused. Then they calmly walked into the room. "Adelle? Where are you hiding, darling?"

The footsteps were along the far wall. They moved to the center of the room. "Are you under the bed?"

Bed? The room is empty... Katie realized that in this alternate reality, she was back in time and the bed was once again there for the family. *Of course.*

John walked up beside the paneling. He was mere inches from Katie and Adelle. Could he not know of this secret hiding spot? Evidently not.

The footsteps walked towards the door to the hall. "Adelle? Where are you?"

Suddenly Adelle reached out and slid the panel open wide, exposing both her and Katie. Katie was in shock. She grabbed at Adelle but her hands seemed to pass through her.

Adelle ran around the corner out of sight. "Daddy! Why are you mad at us? Wake up, Daniel..."

Another shot. Silence.

Oh my God. Adelle. That sweet innocent soul. The taste of vomit was in Katie's mouth. She felt sick. *I can't stay here, I've got to save Elizabeth.*

Even Katie was surprised at the sudden rush of confidence. Fearlessness.

Katie climbed out of the hiding spot and ran into the hall. Lying face up was Daniel. Two shots to his chest. She turned left to see Adelle lying face down in a pool of blood. Her hair and scalp were torn off from a bullet to the head.

Rage filled Katie. She thundered down the stairs, her left shoulder hitting the wall as she was rushing so fast.

She ran into the living room, expecting to meet John for a confrontation.

He wasn't there. The front door was wide open. The smell of smoldering kindling came from the fireplace. She looked to the right and once again saw Agnes lying face down. A massive pool of blood lay under her.

Katie looked out the doorway to see John walking towards Elizabeth. Elizabeth was crumpled up under the willow tree. She looked like she was crying.

Katie rushed out the front door towards John. When she reached him, she grabbed his arm. Only her hand went right through him.

"John. Don't do this. Please. Don't do this. This is making God angry."

John kept walking. His face was expressionless and his eyes were... indescribable. The whites of his eyes could only be described as red. They seemed to glow under the reflection of the sunlight.

John calmly walked up to Elizabeth and stopped a few feet from her.

"Elizabeth, run!" Katie whimpered.

Elizabeth looked up defiantly. "Mom was right. Your obsession with religion will destroy us all. You won't silence us, Dad. We will haunt you for eternity—"

John calmly raised his gun and shot Elizabeth dead. Just as calmly as you would change a channel on a television remote, he simply turned her life off. Just like that. Calmly. Coldly.

"Time to clean up," John said. He put the gun into the waistband of his pants, reached down and picked up Elizabeth like a sack of potatoes. He turned and headed into the house. He dropped her body—not placed it, dropped it —onto the floor by her mother.

He walked to the kitchen and placed his gun calmly back in its box. He closed the lid. He turned off the light and walked out the kitchen door.

Beside the back door was a wooden box filled with rags and gas cans. John set a rag alight and dropped it into the box. It smoldered for a bit and then set fire to the other rags. His face was expressionless.

Little did John know that the fire would damage the back wall, but wouldn't have its desired effect. It would burn out by itself, causing only cosmetic damage. Ironically, another failure for John.

Katie watched him as he walked off towards the woods, eventually disappearing into the bushes. He had nothing but the clothes on his back. It would be the last anyone saw of John, assuming that Katie was truly seeing him.

Unfortunately, that would not be the last Katie saw of John.

CHAPTER EIGHTEEN

Katie gasped for air as though she'd been underwater too long. She sat up in her bed, terrified.

It was a dream. It was a dream, she told herself. I hate these damn dreams. They are driving me bonkers-

Something was wrong. Katie took a deep sniff and realized she was smelling smoke. Faint, but there. She shook her head. She was just dreaming of a fireplace smoldering.

The fire was out when I came to bed. I'm certain of it.

Katie quickly turned on the light. A cloud of smoke was slowly rolling along the hallway floor. Jumping out of bed, Katie approached the doorway. Red and orange flickering light illuminated the staircase and the smoke was getting fuller with each second. She was trapped.

I can make it down, around the corner and out the back, she thought. But reason kicked in. That fire appeared to be right at the bottom of the steps. And the smoke was getting heavier by the second.

Just as she was about to turn away, she saw a shadow move.

"Is anyone there?" Katie called out. Of course not, idiot, you're home alone.

Katie slammed the bedroom door shut. She ran and grabbed the duvet and tossed it at the bottom of the door to keep the smoke from coming in the gap.

She stood up and heard a voice say, "Run!"

She jumped in fright. Turning quickly, she was startled to see Daniel standing by the window. Clear as day.

"Dad is angry. You have to get out. Run."

Katie ran to the window. Daniel stood by her and watched. It felt as though he was keeping guard. She frantically wiggled the levers and flung the window open. This was an old house and she was two floors up. She'd break her back jumping.

Daniel encouraged her, as though he could read her mind. "Climb out and run to the back. There's the tool shed, jump on that and then down. It's easy. You can do it."

Katie pulled up a chair, stepped on it and out the window. Daniel stood and watched. With both feet on the roof, she looked back at him. He smiled.

Katie couldn't run. The roof tiles were sloped and too slippery. The opposite side of the house was now glowing, as was the front corner. Flames were jumping out of the chimney. There was no time to waste.

Sure enough, Daniel was right. At the back corner of the house was a tool shed. It was only a four-foot drop.

Katie paused, took a breath and jumped. She landed on the top of the shed but slipped. The roof was pointed to match the points of the house, and in her miscalculation she fell sideways and slid off the roof completely. She landed on the ground on her left leg with a sharp twist and an angry smack.

"Ahhhhh!" she screamed. Her left foot was in excruciating pain. Sprained? Broken? She didn't know and didn't care as her ribs hurt so bad that it was almost impossible to breathe.

"I'm too close to the house. Move it, bitch," she said to herself.

She stood up with great difficulty. Her foot was screaming pain signals to her brain. With most of her weight on her right foot she hopped her way to the front of the house. Smoke was everywhere and seemed to follow her every move. She was coughing and gagging, working to get away.

"Oh my God. I left my phone and keys upstairs!" Katie cried out. She hustled as fast as she could to the car. *Did I leave the valet key in the glove box?*

Bad habits can pay off. Notorious for never locking her doors, she swung the door open and sat in the driver's seat. The relief of taking the weight off of her left foot was incredible.

Katie leaned over and frantically opened the glove box, pulling out tissues, parking tickets, speeding tickets and other useless bits of junk. No key.

Katie sat back up and punched the steering wheel. She watched in horror as the library and lower half of the house were engulfed in flames. Daniel was standing at the window, watching. Behind him was a faint red and orange glow.

The armrest. Katie twisted to open the car armrest. She reached down and fumbled her fingers around and found... the valet key.

She pulled her legs into the car and slammed the door shut, banging her foot on the brake pedal, sending a searing jolt of pain up her leg. Katie jammed the key into the ignition and cranked it. The engine fired up and she put the car into reverse. As she pulled away she looked up at the bedroom. Daniel was gone.

But John stood watching. She shook her head and refocused her eyes, and flames engulfed her curtains and fire roared out the open window.

Katie raced down the long private road to the main highway, turned left and put the pedal to the metal. In her heart of hearts she knew there was no saving the house. But she had to make an effort.

Slow down, girl, you're going to kill yourself, she thought. Her tires were squealing on corners that were particularly hard. Fortunately, her reputation for being a speeding ticket magnet came true.

"Christmastime," she said out loud. She almost had a squeal of joy in her voice. It was her favorite saying whenever she saw the police lights in the rearview mirror.

Katie hit the brakes and pulled over. She quickly rolled down her window and stuck her hand out, waving violently. She wanted to jump out and run to the police cruiser, but given her foot being injured and police shootings being out of control, she thought it best to stay where she was.

The police officer was walking towards the car cautiously and had his hand on his gun as a precaution.

"Officer, my house is on fire! Please call the fire department!"

"Why didn't you call?" said the officer, looking somewhat skeptical.

"Sir! My phone is in the house, I have no way to contact anyone. Please. Blackstone Manor. It's burning to the ground as we speak."

The officer reached up with his left hand to the walkie-talkie on his shoulder and headed back to his car at a run. Katie was getting very impatient. It was taking too long for her. She put the car and drive and did a U-turn, slowly so as to not alarm the police officer too much. It didn't help; he was already freaking out when she pulled her car to the side of the road across from his.

"Stop! Don't move your car until I say so. If you—"

"My house is burning down. When you figure out how to call the fire department I'm going back to it. Follow me, stay here, I don't care. I'm going back to my house," Katie said.

As she slowly drove away the officer looked furious. His left hand was on the walkie-talkie and he ran back to his car. Maybe he thought she was trying to get away. *Whatever. Come and get me.*

It was only a few moments before the police car was right up on her behind. He was doing that annoying squawking with the siren but she ignored it. She had four-way flashers on, and wasn't driving fast or doing anything dangerous. She figured he was probably going to ram her off the road. Fine.

She turned right onto the private road that led up the big hill to the house. The police car gave out one last squawk and then slowed down briefly.

The next thing Katie knew the siren was on and he raced past her up the hill. At this point the flames could be seen a good mile away, she estimated.

She rolled in right behind him, parking close to the willow tree. Not thinking, she swung open the door and jumped out. Being in the car and having a massive adrenaline rush had made her forget about the pain in her foot. When she jumped out a massive surge raced up her leg and she collapsed to the ground.

The officer rushed over. "Are you okay? Is there anyone in the house? Any pets in the house?" The questions came fast and her answers shot back fast.

"Yes, no, no."

"What happened to your leg?"

"I jumped off the roof."

"Wow. I'm surprise you still have a spine!" he said, grabbing his shoulder walkie-talkie. "Need ambulance to Blackstone Manor, possible fractured leg, over." Then, to her, "Let me get you back in the car."

"No. It hurts too much. I need to stretch it out. Can you please just rest me up against the willow?"

"Sure thing," he said. He grabbed her left arm and put it around his shoulder and helped her hop to the willow. He wasn't particularly gentle; he was more military-like in function.

"I'm going to leave you here for a moment. I gotta move your car out of the way for the fire department, and then move mine further over. We've got at least two trucks coming," he said. He didn't even wait for an acknowledgement. *Terrible bedside manner,* she thought, half-laughing.

The house was totally engulfed in flames. They were at a safe enough distance and yet close enough that the slight breeze brought waves of heat.

"You got your way, Blackstone. You destroyed everything. Your house could have brought so much joy to so many, you evil bastard..."

Katie leaned back on the willow. Her left leg seemed to radiate pain with every heartbeat. Her ribs were sore as hell and her arms were scraped. She gazed down at her chest and noticed fresh blood—a lot of it.

She took her right hand and looked down her shirt. Her chest was fine. Neck, fine. She touched her chin and it was dripping wet. She tucked her chin into the neck of her shirt and compressed the cut. *Must have gotten it during the fall,* she thought.

How attractive I must have been to the police officer. He must have thought I was in a zombie movie. She laughed. But it hurt.

Katie sat in daze, watching her house burn to the ground. She watched in morbid fascination as the 'third' floor collapsed. Everything seemed in slow motion.

Fire trucks groaned up the hill. The fire chief arrived first. The officer ran over to him immediately and telegraphed the situation, "No people, no pets," and the fire chief yelled out to his crew, "Contain it."

The crew got to work fast. They were worried about the trees behind the house and seemed to focus their attention there.

An ambulance ambled its way up and parked close to the tree. A woman came to Katie's aid, and quickly assessed a broken ankle. She and her partner put on a temporary brace and lifted her to the stretcher.

Other than a bad cut on the chin, which they bandaged, she was otherwise just badly banged up.

A tall, lanky police officer looked into the back of the ambulance. "A Miss Mel Wragg wants you to know she'll meet you at the hospital—"

"Is she okay?"

"Uh, yes, I believe so. Her car broke down, and she has been at the dealership all day."

"Thank you." Katie winced. Her foot was getting worse.

As they drove away, she looked out the back windows at the house and the lonely willow tree and wondered what story the willow would tell if it could talk.

CHAPTER NINETEEN

13 months later...

"Hey chickie! How are you?"

"I'm doing fantastic, Mel! How are you doing?"

"I've got some amazing news for you. You will not believe it when I tell you —"

"Don't keep me in suspense! I hate that," Katie said, laughing.

"First, tell me how things are going for you in Seattle and that house flip?"

Katie was actually standing in the living room of the house in Bellevue, Washington. A weathered and badly neglected 2500 square foot home on a huge piece of land, she transformed it into a thing of beauty. She was beaming as she spoke on the phone.

"I'm putting the 'for sale' sign on the front lawn as we speak. House is complete, and it looks amazing. Very profitable flip, almost everything was cosmetic, so it was a fast and easy fix—"

"Profitable?" Mel interrupted.

"Oh, dear lord, yes. I'll clear fifty thousand on this one for less than a month of work—"

"Holy crap. That's incredible. How do—"

"What's the news? I'm dying here." Katie decided it was a perfect time to celebrate. She went to the kitchen and pulled out a plastic drinking glass, a bottle of Merlot and a bottle opener.

"Well, I was going to suggest you grab a glass but clearly you are well ahead of me. Get ready for this: they found John Blackstone."

Katie froze. There was silence for what seemed like an eternity. "Found him? What do you mean?"

"Hikers were going through the woods and saw something weird, apparently. They found what looked like a campsite and a collapsed tent. Old. They checked it out and found human remains inside—"

"Oh my God. How do they know it's him and—"

"They found a stash of old money. Like, the old style from years ago—"

"I get it, Mel. Answer the question! How'd they know it was him?" Katie said. She gulped down about half the plastic cup of wine. As she put the cup on the counter, her hand was trembling.

"They found his identification on him. I didn't get all the details, but they found his wedding ring I know for sure and some other identifiers—"

"Where? Where was he from the house—"

"Katie. Calm down. Please. You're starting to sound upset—"

"The bastard tried to kill me."

"He's dead now. For sure. His house is gone. I'm sure he's finished with his time here in this dimension, chickie," Mel said. She tried to sound soothing and reassuring.

"Mel. WHERE?"

"He was about two miles away from what would have been the back door of your house."

Katie stood silently. It was raining, after all, this was Washington. She looked out the window at the big back yard through the water streaked glass. A chill ran through her.

"They are sure it was him?"

"You know I've got connections with the police. They haven't officially got forensics back, I just wanted you to know."

Katie shuddered and decided it would be best to change the topic. She wanted nothing to do with that house and the whole fiasco freaked her out. She changed the topic to their upcoming trip to Mexico for a week of "partying and debauchery" as Mel called it. The trip was only weeks away.

After a bit of gossip, Mel said goodbye. Katie hung up, sealed up her wine and drove back to her small condo downtown. Beautiful, and just a few blocks from the famous Pike's Place.

Katie reopened her bottle of wine and poured another glass, in a proper and sophisticated wine glass. She took a swig and headed to her hall closet. On the floor was a cardboard file box labeled 'Blackstone Manor' on it. She picked it up and carried it to the living room, placing it on the coffee table. She tossed the cardboard lid onto the floor and started pulling out the contents.

Out came the file folder with all the legal documents, results of the investigation and insurance claim. The sale of the land to the next owner, a developer.

But these weren't the things she was looking for.

"Where are you?" Katie said out loud.

Buried at the bottom of the box was a ziplock plastic bag. Found you, she thought, grabbing it and placing it on the couch.

Taking a deep breath, Katie felt the need for some 'medicine.' She got up, retrieved her glass of wine and bottle and sat back on the couch. She poured a very full glass of wine and sat back.

The fire chief has visited Katie in the hospital the following morning of the fire. As she lay in the hospital bed with a huge bandage on her chin to protect the stitches and her leg in a cast, he asked her only a few questions.

Before he left, he said they found something strange in the rubble. A book. More accurately, a Bible. The black leather had been singed and the edges of the pages scorched. He gave it to her as a 'souvenir.'

That Bible was in the bag that she was gently fingering with her right hand, as she slurped the wine. The memories and the horror were still there in her mind, clear as if it were last night.

Suddenly placing the glass down she pulled the ziplock open with a surge of curiosity. The air filled with the scent of burned wood, still strong after all this time.

How the hell did this survive— she froze for a second and then burst out laughing at the fact she said 'hell' holding a Bible. It was a nervous laugh.

Charred dust was falling from the Bible. It was dropping onto the rug and her couch. Didn't plan this out too well, she thought, placing it on the coffee table.

Katie carefully opened the Bible, it's cover barely attached due to the damage and the first few pages fell out. The first page that she saw was the "Presentation" page. In thick black ink, it simply read, BLACKSTONE.

It had an inscription. It was very faded. Katie leaned close to it and tilted her head to read it. It read:

To Agnes,
May you live ten years longer than I,
and may I never die.
Love, John.

Katie sat back on the couch. A chill ran through her.

May I never die? Katie thought. She let out a weak laugh and put the Bible back in its bag and got up from the couch. You better be dead, she thought, raising her glass of wine in a toast.

"May your family rest in peace and may you burn in hell for eternity, John."

As Katie chugged the last of her wine, she gazed out at the darkened city lit by street lights and signs. The rain was now drizzling softly and she enjoyed the quiet and the darkness...

Scratch scratch scratch. Scratch scratch. Silence. Scratch scratch scratch.

AUTHOR NOTES

GET A FREE COLLECTION OF SIX SHORT GHOST STORIES

Building a relationship with my readers is the very best thing about writing. I occasionally send newsletters with details on new releases, special offers and other bits of news relating to hauntings and thrillers.

Sign up right now and be the FIRST to hear about all activities and releases. Please visit www.JamesM-Matheson.com for more details.

Enjoy this book? You can make a big difference

I sincerely hope you enjoyed my book. If you did, please consider leaving a brief review on Amazon. Reviews are my most powerful secret to spreading the word.

I'm proud of the fact that I have a large list of loyal readers. I don't have the budget that the big publishing houses have, but I do have you.

Please leave a review wherever you purchased this book from.

Thank you in advance for doing so.

ABOUT THE AUTHOR

James M. Matheson is a storyteller. His grade seven class took a trip to a northern pioneer village. On talent night he shared a story about a table possessed by spirits that terrified his classmates. He has written and told scary stories ever since. He lives in the southwest USA with his wife.

CPSIA information can be obtained
at www.ICGtesting.com
Printed in the USA
LVOW13s1500250117

522153LV00009B/634/P